Queen

By Ebony

Diamonds

Queen Malone

I sat at my dining room table and sipped down my glass of 2006 Lafite-Rothschild Bordeaux. It was an eight-thousand-dollar bottle that I only drank when I was feeling especially sexy.

"Mmmmmmmmmmm, yeeesss." I picked up my fork and began to eat my Caesar salad before diving into my shrimp/crab alfredo. My body jumped in pleasure, and I smiled but continued to eat.

I raised my leg over the Rosewood dining chair arm and looked down at Perry, who was eating my pussy while I ate my food. Sometimes I did this so I could enjoy my food on a different level. I heard that sex enhances the taste buds.

"Eat your dinner, nigga."

I came in his mouth and kicked him away with my new Valentino Rockstud heels. My body felt so good that I hated the sight of him afterward, even though he was sexy as hell. I didn't want his dick, and that was what irritated me the most.

"Thank you. You can leave," I told him, and I ate the last bite of my food.

"Thank you."

He left the dining room, and I got up and went to the den, which was adjacent to the formal dining room, and sat behind the desk. I pulled out the white gold strain of weed that I had in the desk drawer and snatched a sheet out of the cardboard Bob Marley hemp and began to roll up after breaking the weed down.

I lived in a seventeen thousand square foot mansion in Miami on North Bay Road. My backyard was Biscayne Bay, and I had an infinity pool built at a ledge that fell in the bay. I looked out at the city lights and smiled.

"Queen." Tevony, my assistant, walked in.

"Yeah." I turned around, and she looked at me like she didn't wanna say whatever she was disturbing me for.

"He got shot," she said with a quivering lip.

I felt my blood literally boiling.

"Is he dead?" I asked and looked back out the window.

"No, he's in the hospital."

"Then why the fuck you here when you need to be putting out the hit!" I yelled at her, and she ran off.

I hadn't talked to Wessie Rain in two and a half years, and I missed him every single one of those days. He was my greatest love after Base. I always watched him from afar through one of my henchmen, well, henchwomen. I only had female muscle. Everyone who worked directly for me was a female, drivers, security, and even my chefs, shit. All bad bitches too. I made the mistake a few years ago of hiring men and had to kill them all, but that's another story.

"Wessie," I said aloud, letting a single tear fall from my eye and wiping it away just as quick.

You didn't fuck with a queen's diamonds or gold, and this nigga was both to me. I would cause a war about him, and the streets knew that so who the fuck would be stupid enough to try me like this? I hated when I had to flex my power. I'd rather have peace, but in times like this, I had to show motherfuckers who was the queen in Miami.

We must go back to how I got here. How can a woman be the biggest dope dealer in Miami? She worked her ass off in these nasty ass streets until her fingers bled, and her body felt broken. That bitch went through broken glass without a scratch, and now that bitch was worth more than 380 million dollars legally, and dirty money was making that look like a Payless shoe to a red bottom. Who is that bitch?

Me, I'm that bitch.

Fourteen years ago

"Mommy, why I gotta wear TJ's draws?" I looked up at my mother, who had tears in her eyes now.

"I ain't have no money to get y'all new school clothes, I'm sorry." She wiped her face.

TJ was my brother, and he was a year older than me.

"You need to be grateful for what you got, bitch." My father came in the room high as a kite.

I was only eight years old, and he was so evil, especially when he was on this shit. Crack had become his family, and we just existed.

"Don't you talk to my daughter like that, muthafucka," my mother snarled.

"You a bitch too." He spit in her face.

"Oh, yeah?" She pulled the blade from her bra and sliced him right across his face.

"Come on, nigga," she said as TJ grabbed me and pulled me into the corner.

"Get the fuck outta here, you damn junkie!" Ma screamed as he ran out.

"I hate him."

I looked at him in total disgust as I told myself that I would never be with a man like my father when I grow up. I watched my mother hustle and move to take care of us, all while fist fighting and shit with my father. I hated to see her hurt, and I always thought about taking the pain from her.

"Don't say that." She smacked me. "He's still your father."

All day at school, I thought about the movie I saw where the woman killed her husband by putting stuff in his food. So, later that night, I sat in my room eating when I heard my father come in, begging for my mother's forgiveness yet again. Of course, she accepted his apology. We ate dinner, and my father called out for me to bring him a beer like he often did.

When I went to the kitchen, I saw dish detergent and wondered if this would do the trick. I poured some in his beer and grabbed ammonia from the cabinet and poured it in too. The smell was bad, and I hoped he drank it before he could notice.

"Here." I handed it to him.

"Good, lil' bitch, now go finish your homework." He pushed me backward, away from his TV view. He took a huge gulp, and his eyes bulged as he wheezed for air.

"Richie, what's wrong?" My mother ran up to him as he started to convulse.

She called the ambulance, and they whisked him away. He never made it back; his lungs collapsed. Even at my young age, I didn't play with niggas, not even my own father. What I didn't expect was for the hospital to figure out what happened, and my mother was charged with his murder. I didn't know how to tell anybody that I was the one, so I lost my mother too. That hurt me, especially since it was my fault.

We ended up living with Aunt Bella, my mother's older sister in Liberty City. She looked like Hattie from *Amen*, size and all. She cooked so good, I started to gain weight from all the soul food and cakes. She was a beast in the kitchen, and she was strict as hell. It was okay when we were younger, but as we got into our teens, she got worse. She would always say that she didn't want us caught up in the streets, but we stayed like most teens did.

I was sixteen when I realized why she didn't want us out there because the streets ain't have love for no fucking body. I learned that in the worst way, and it changed me. One day, I was walking home from school with my friend, Bevie, and her cousin, Shadesah, when we saw police and ambulances rushing down the street. Since we lived in Pork and Beans, of course, that was a daily activity around here, so it didn't move us.

On some real shit, growing up around there, I easily became a product of my environment. I saw people smoke, so I smoked, I saw my friends fucking, so I fucked. I used to wish myself out of the projects, but that shit was for the birds when I got old enough to realize you had to make some shit shake on your own.

I started to look for TJ as soon as I got to my building to make sure he was okay. He had started to move a little something despite my aunt's warnings and attempts to scare us straight. He was drawn to the shit, and he was coming up around here.

When I got upstairs to check if he was home, the apartment was empty, but the TV was on Sanford and Son, which my Aunt watched religiously.

"Aunt Bella!" I called out with no response.

I left and went toward the spot she and her friends sit and drink at sometimes, but I stopped when I heard screaming in the distance.

"Not him! Not him!" It sounded like my aunt screaming. The voice was hoarse but definitely sounded like her.

"Man, I'm sorry," Romeo, one of my friends, said.

"What?" I saw my aunt on the ground with the police surrounding her.

"You can't take him," she screamed.

When I approached, I saw TJ lying dead in her arms with his head riddled with bullets. His face had holes everywhere.

"They did that man dirty," I heard someone say in the crowd.

I was still and in shock from seeing my brother like that; I couldn't even shed a tear.

"Queen!" My aunt grabbed me when the police pulled my brother from her arms.

"Why y'all do him like this?" I broke my silence and screamed at the crowd. "Who the fuck killed my brother?" I looked at all the onlookers. "Yeah, I know, no snitchin', right? Fuck all y'all." I pushed past them motherfuckers and went in the house then turned the shower on steaming hot.

I got in, and the water burned my skin so bad. Finally, I started to cry.

"No, TJ, why, bro?" I sat on the floor of the tub and let the water rush over me. I wasn't here until 5 in the morning and the water had started run cold long ago. I didn't want to go into reality.

A few months later, life seemed to be going back to normal, even though my heart was ripped out from TJ's death. It was getting easier to deal with as time went on. I was doing better in school and decided to occupy my time by joining the cheerleading squad. I just couldn't be home no more after that and tried anything to get there when it was time for bed. My mother was eaten up inside that those bastards wouldn't even let her out for the funeral. I blamed myself because that shit was my fault.

"Now you know its Nationals in a month, and this sloppy shit y'all doing not finna cut it," our cheerleading and gym coach, Ms. Deverson, said.

"Her ugly ass stay talking shit like she can even do the moves," Parquita, the captain, spat as Ms. Deverson walked away.

"Okay, so I do think we need to work on the jumps and the coordination with the dance. Martisa, you just be all over the place," I said.

"I ain't the only one, Queen. Why the fuck you gotta point me out?" Martisa pushed her glasses up and folded her arms.

"Because you the worst," I said, and everybody laughed.

"Aight, Queen," Parquita said, and I shrugged.

"I don't know how you became co-captain, but this some ole bullshit," Martisa said and walked away.

"Your ass is mean." Parquita looked at me with a smirk.

"No, her ass retarded and blind."

I picked up my bag and put my windbreaker on. We had storms, and shit had been windy and wet for the last few days.

"Damn, I wish my father could come to get me." Parquita pulled out her phone and went through it.

"I need me a damn phone. My aunt says she might gimme one next week," I told her.

"Good, then we can talk longer and be textin'."

She pushed through the exit doors, and I saw the dude who always stood out front by the basketball courts selling weed and shit. He was leaning on this old school Cutlass, and it was clean as hell.

"That's where I got that weed from the other day that you said was fire." Parquita pointed to him.

"Oh, for real? I thought you got it from Eric again," I said as I watched the guy collect money.

"His name is Tonka. My brother is friends with him." Parquita walked up to dude like it was nothing, and I followed her.

"Hey, Tonka." Parquita hugged him.

"Wassup, shawty?" he said to her then looked at me.

His grills were iced out, and the studs in his ears were shining bright. I loved his waves with his low cut. Damn, he was fine.

"Wuz good, lil' mama." He looked at me, and I slapped hands with him and dapped him up like niggas do.

For some reason, he burst out laughing, even holding his stomach. He turned to a dude who was standing behind him.

"You see shawty?" He pointed at me.

"I see, she ain't friendly with them hugs," the dude spoke and pulled smoke through his blunt.

"I just don't know you to be huggin' on a nigga and shit."

"Okay, okay, you smart." Tonka nodded and looked me up and down.

"This TJ's sister," the nigga said behind him, and it made me wonder how the fuck he knew that.

"Oh, word? I'm sorry to hear about what happened to him," Tonka said, and I felt more at ease that he was cool with TJ.

"Thanks." I nodded.

"You think I can get some more of that shit from the other day? We was just speakin' on it." Parquita used her thumb to point at me.

"Y'all lil' asses don't need to be smokin'." He reached his hand back, and dude handed him a nice sack.

"You want some too?" Tonka asked me, but his tone was more like 'you want some of me.'

"I ain't got no money," I said, and he stuffed a bag in my hand.

"It's on me." He touched his chest.

"Damn, its rainin' now." I looked at the raindrop that landed on my hand.

"Yeah, we finna move out. Y'all need a ride?" Tonka asked.

"Hell yeah." Parquita waved me on, and we hopped in his car.

I felt nervous for some reason around him. He seemed so powerful.

"You stay in Pork 'n Beans too?" Tonka asked me, and I nodded.

"Cool." He turned his music up, and we rode and smoked with them until we got to the block.

"Aye, step out real fast, and let me holla at baby girl," Tonka said to Parquita and the dude he was with.

I got out, and he patted the passenger seat for me to get in.

"What's your name?" he asked, and I felt like I was on fire.

"Queen." I looked at him, and the eye he gave me, I had never seen before.

"I like that." He licked his lips.

"How old is you?" he asked.

"Sixteen."

"Oh, okay. I just turned nineteen. You got a lil nigga chasin' after you?" he asked me, and I giggled.

"I had a boyfriend, but we broke up. He a clown." I thought about Jamal's punk ass.

"Fuck that nigga. Gimme yo' number." He handed me his phone, and I gave him the house number.

When I turned to get out, he pulled me to him and kissed me.

"You gon' be my shorty, so make sure you go get your hair done and shit. Ion like that lil' ponytail shit on your head." He handed me a knot of money, and my eyes grew wide.

"I can't take this shit," I told him.

"Why not? Go get your shit straight, and I'ma call you tonight." He nodded.

"Okay," I simply said and got out.

"Aw, bitch, did Tonka just kiss you?" Parquita asked.

"Yeah." I blushed.

"Girl, I hope Qia don't find out," she said, and I snapped my neck.

"Who?" I asked her.

"His girlfriend. I know you ain't think no nigga like that was single." She laughed.

"Man, fuck." I pushed the money in my pocket and decided to spend it and say fuck him. I ain't no side chick, just because I'm young, and niggas think that means we stupid.

Over the next few days, I let my aunt tell Tonka I wasn't home, and I would go out the other exit from school, so he wouldn't see me. I thought I was slick until he came into the gym while we were practicing.

"Tonka, what the hell?" Parquita looked confused.

"Aye, shorty, I need to holla at chu," Tonka said to me, ignoring Parquita.

"Young man, this school is for students, and right now, we're practicing." Ms. Deverson approached him.

"Bitch, get the fuck out my face. Your breath is real live offensive." Tonka covered his nose.

"I'm getting security." Ms. Deverson walked off.

"Come on," he barked at me.

I looked at the girls then walked up to him, and he pulled me out the back door.

"Why the fuck your hair not done, and why the fuck you got your people lyin' to me?" he asked.

"I ain't got nobody lyin'," I said in a childlike tone.

"You is. Why the fuck you tryna play a nigga like me?"

"I ain't. You tried to play me. I know you got a girl," I said, and he shook his head.

"Parquita told you that?" he asked me, and I nodded. "You know what? I can't fuck wit chu." He started to walk away.

"Nigga, what? You the one on bullshit, and you can't fuck wit' me? Tuh."

"Yeah, I can't because you never let no bitch tell you about your nigga, and you obviously will believe everything a hoe say."

"Nigga, do you got a girl?" I asked.

"Yeah, I do, but that's not the point. You should have told her to mind her fuckin' business and fucked wit' me," he said in a serious tone.

This nigga confused me with that shit.

"But you do got a girl, so we cool anyway." I chucked him the deuce.

"Tell me to dump her ass, and I'll call her right now," he said.

I looked at him and giggled.

"You met me days ago, and you really think I believe you would dump your girl?" I shook my head.

"I ain't never lied to no bitch, so if I say it's truth, it's truth. Fuck you wanna do?" He pulled his phone out.

"Do it then, nigga," I called his bluff.

He hit some buttons, and I could hear that he had it on speaker.

"Hey, boo." Some girl picked up.

"Aye, I got this new girl I'm fuckin' wit. Don't call my phone again, Qia."

"Tonka, what the fuck you mean? What bitch?" The girl sounded traumatized by what he'd just said.

"That's not nice," I said, realizing how mean it was.

"Wait, that bitch right there? I'ma kill that bitch," she spat, and the phone died.

"She mad." Tonka shook his head.

"Nigga, you just dumped her, and in front of a bitch. I would be mad too. You need to apologize," I said.

"You already tryna tell me what to do, girl." He backed me into the wall.

"No, but still. Right is right."

I looked down, and he pulled my chin up, then slid his tongue across my lips. I gasped when he kissed me. He completely took my breath away.

"He probably ran out here," I heard Ms. Deverson say.

"You gotta go," I told him.

"You better be the fuck in the house to answer the phone." He jogged off, and the door opened as soon as he hit the corner.

"Are you okay? Where did that fool go?" Ms. Deverson asked.

"I'm okay. We friends and got into a little fight. It's okay," I assured her.

"No, we calling the police. Did he touch you?"

"I said he ain't do shit," I repeated and looked at the chunky security guard who stood there.

"Y'all lil' fast ass girls ain't never gonna learn." Ms. Deverson walked away.

I wanted to beat her ass, but I showed restraint.

When I got home, two girls were standing out front who I'd never seen before.

"Aye, is you Queen?" One of them walked up.

"Why?" I asked.

"Because, bitch, I was the one on the phone when you was wit' my nigga. Yeah, word carried that you been sniffin' 'round him and shit," she said.

"I don't know what the fuck you talkin' 'bout, but you need to step the fuck up off my porch," I said, not backing down, even though the shit literally just happened an hour ago.

"Bitch, I'm Qia, Tonka's girlfriend. Wait, how old is this lil' bitch?" she said, looking at her friend.

"Girl, Jayricka on the team with her and was there when Tonka came up in there," the chick responded and mugged me.

"Oh, you a young bitch? I should slap the fuck out you for being grown!" Qia said.

"You can try." I dropped my bookbag.

"Queen, what's goin' on?" Ms. Tisha, my friend Gabby's mother, came up.

"This ain't none of ya business. This lil bitch out here tryna fuck my nigga, and she finna get her ass whooped," Qia said.

"You ain't touchin' her. You ever think your man don't want you?" Ms. Tisha spat back.

"He dumped her already," I said, and that set Qia off.

She caught me one good time, and I came back strong. Ms. Tisha was beating her friend up while I fought Qia.

"Queen, what the hell?" Aunt Bella came out and pulled me off Qia.

I felt my face burning, so I knew the bitch had scratched me.

"Why you out there fighting?" Aunt Bella asked as she pulled me into the house.

"That bitch ran up on me," I spat, still angry.

"For what, Queen?" she slapped her hand on her thigh.

"Tonka, she's his ex," I told her.

"See, that fool already got you in some shit. I told you he's gonna bring you down, Queen. Soon as I heard about him kissing you the other day." She shook her finger in my face.

"No, he won't, Aunt Bella. He can't stop his ex from approaching me," I told her and walked into my room and sat on the bed. I was gonna snap on him when he called.

I waited for the call, which never came, and I felt like a fucking idiot. He played the shit out of me, and all I could do was laugh. When midnight came around, I rolled a blunt and went downstairs to smoke out front so I could just get air and relax.

I watched people walk up and down the street as I smoked, thinking about how fucked up dudes could be, but when I saw who was coming toward me, my mood changed.

"You must have known I was comin'." Tonka sat next to me.

"Nah, I didn't. I was about to be ghost on you again."

"Yeah, aight, you learned your lesson. I got into some shit and had to move around, so I tossed my phone and got a new one. I ain't know your shit by heart." He ran his hand down my leg.

"What the fuck happened to your face?" he asked.

"Your fuckin' girl came over here. This bitch I cheer with told her where I live."

"Man, she stupid as shit, mane," he said.

"Yeah, she is. I beat her ass too, so you need to get her in line, Tonka. I don't need this shit," I told him.

"Okay, I got chu. I'm sorry." He kissed me.

"It's cool. I'm glad you pulled up," I admitted.

"Shit, me too. I wanted to continue what we had goin' on," he said, and I shook my head.

"Nope. I ain't no easy chick, nigga."

"I ain't say you was, but keep that attitude up." He chuckled.

We sat out front and smoked blunt after blunt until some niggas started shooting and fucked up our vibe, so we went to his car. I liked him a lot, and it was no faking about it. He talked about his mother and father, which was a fucked-up story. His mother got killed by the police after they killed his father. She busted at them, and they took her out too. I told him about my past, but I left out who really killed my father. I never told him what my mother was even in jail for.

Before he left, we kissed in his car for a while before I got out and ran in the house then and lay in my bed thinking. I had already daydreamed of us being together and getting married, all in that moment. After days of barely knowing each or even talking but three times and this nigga had me feeling like this. Damn. I knew I was young, but I was ready.

We dove headfirst into our relationship, and Tonka was showing me real love. I stayed in the latest shit, and he even got me my own little car. Girls at school watched me with envy now. I quit cheerleading to spend all my time with him. I started to sit and watch him sling all his dope and even moved some shit myself. The first time we had sex, I thought I was in another world, and I had been addicted to him ever since.

When my mother heard about it from my aunt, she called for me to come to see her.

***

This was the first time in a year that I had been to the prison. I stopped going because she always seemed to not be interested in seeing me. When we would go, she would just look at me and answer yes or no. That shit made me uncomfortable.

"Step through," the officer told me, and I headed to the visiting room.

When I saw my mother, she looked better than I expected, and she actually had a smile on her face.

"Hey, Mama." I hugged her.

She pulled back and looked at me.

"You so fucking stupid, Queen." She shook her head and sat down.

"Huh?" I looked at her like she was crazy with that mood swing.

"You let that nigga get you pregnant," she spat loudly, and everyone looked at me as the room got quiet.

"I'm not pregnant, Ma. What the fuck you doin'?" I asked, wondering why she would embarrass me like this.

"I can tell. I smell it on you. You gonna ruin your life, Queen. Your aunt told me he was some low life dope dealer, and you dressing like you spending legit money. Look at you." She pointed to my jewelry and my Fendi outfit.

"Wow. I ain't comin' back." I was about to walk away.

"I let you put me in here. The least you could do is take advantage of what I gave you. Life and freedom," she said, and that caused me to become frozen in place.

She came up to my ear. "I know you killed him, Queen," she said.

I cried and ran out of the room. My heart was pounding out of my chest, and I didn't know what to do.

I was scared of what she said and how she said it. It was terrifying. I drove away and never went back to see her. She was right about one thing, though, I was pregnant by Tonka, and I was scared shitless.

She wrote me a letter that she was getting out, and the same summer, I moved in with Tonka. Here I was, sixteen and pregnant by a drug dealer. I ain't see that shit coming.

Three years later

"Dumb ass bitch!" Tonka punched me right in the nose, and my blood sprayed out like a shaken soda can.

I hit him in the chin and got him with two more shots. He backhanded me, and that shit dazed me.

"Aye, nigga, that's enough." Tonka's friend, Base, ran up and pushed him away.

"No, this bitch in there talking to some nigga when I went to the bathroom," he hollered and tried to get at me.

I had my fist up, ready for his ass. I was no punk bitch, and he knew that shit.

"He was the fuckin' bartender! He asked me what I wanted to drink," I cried, but not from hurt, from the fact that I might murder this nigga tonight.

"And you know to wait 'til I come back, bitch, so I can tell him." He kicked me off the barstool, and I hit my head when I landed.

He was fucked up drunk, and I hated when he got like that because I had to go round for round, but I held my own.

"Fuck you, nigga. On my father, you a bitch." I cried at how humiliating this shit was.

He did this all the time, and I was weary of the shit. We had been together off and on over the years, and this year was the biggest mistake of my life for not killing him when I had the chance.

Tonka was perfect all through my last two years of high school and was a good ass father when it came to our son. I mean, he was supportive and showered me with love and anything I could ever want. He even fully introduced me to the drug game, and I learned how to cook and eyeball weight. After a while, he would bring me to re-ups and let me look to see if the weight was right without even touching the shit.

Out of the blue, he started to change. Well, at least how we were changed. When he started to get deeper and deeper into the life, he also became a little mean and seemed like I irritated him most of the time. It got bad as Tadius got older. I gave him TJ's real name and wouldn't have had it any other way. He was four now, and he was the best thing that came from me and Tonka's relationship.

As I walked out of the bar, I heard footsteps behind me. I thought it was Tonka, so I pulled my gun. Fuck it.

"Chill, shorty, it's me." Base came up and slid some keys in my hand.

He was cool and seemed like he shouldn't be around slime like Tonka. He always stopped the shit whenever he was around.

"I hate his ass, Base." I wiped my face and saw blood on my hand.

"You know he drunk as shit," he replied, and I looked at the keys.

"What's this?" I asked.

"Take my car and leave the keys over the tire. Just go 'head home." He walked back inside, and I hit the alarm until I saw the yellow Beamer's lights flash.

I got in and drove away, watching the club disappear in my rearview. I hated this nigga with a passion sometimes. I had decided right at the light that I would pull away from him for good. If he wanted to help me with Tadius, cool, but if not, fuck it. I would start from rock bottom before I kept doing this shit with him.

When I got to Aunt Bella's house that I got her in the grove, of course, the place was pitch black because it was 3:00 in the morning. Tonka had called me a few times, and I ignored him every single time. It wasn't shit but the motions, and I was over it.

I sat in the car for about an hour and a half looking at the house. I knew I couldn't get Tadius at this time of morning. I just didn't wanna go home and wait for this nigga to come in there on his drunk bullshit. I sped away and went home anyway.

When I got there, I saw three cars out front, one of them Tonka's.

"The fuck." I stepped out and heard music blasting from the front windows.

"Go 'head!" I heard a nigga yell as I opened the door.

"Oh, shit. Nigga, yo' bitch home." I heard the same voice, which I now saw was Eddie, one of his friends who was at the club. I didn't see Base, so I figured he was smart and knew how I would react.

Tonka was sitting in the big chair with some bitch on his lap while other bitches danced around.

"I thought you was staying out since you dipped out the club," he smirked, rubbing his hands all over the bitches ass.

"Okay, Tonka, this how we finna play? Let's play, baby. You know I love it."

I looked at him with a huge smile and walked toward the wide white stairs that led to the bedroom. From my closet, I grabbed my choppa. This was it, he was taking the disrespect to another level, so I had to take my rage to the next level. I loaded the clip and saw that I still had blood on my face and nose from when he hit me earlier.

When I walked into the living room, the first girl who saw me screamed at the top of her lungs as I let loose and let the bullets rip through all them bitches and Tonka's friends. I could have sworn I heard laughter until I realized it was me doing the laughing as I laid them all the fuck down, and I realized I was out of my body.

"You stupid ass bitch!" Tonka looked at the mayhem.

"What?" I turned the gun on Tonka. "I ain't hear you, nigga! What the fuck you say, Tonka?" I screamed.

"Oh yeah, Queen, you finna kill me, ma?" he asked, looking like he was scared for his life. He knew he had finally pushed me too far.

"No. Oh, and if you even think about putting your hands on me again, we gon' gun ball, nigga," I spat.

He took a deep breath when I put the gun down.

"What makes you think I won't fuck you up now?" he growled.

"Because I won't be here. I'm leaving, Tonka. You already took up too much of my fuckin' time."

I thought about from when I was sixteen until now. We had serious history, but I had to let it go.

He remained silent as I walked up the stairs and packed two bags. I planned to get my other shit later.

"Queen." Tonka walked into the room as I was walking out.

I quickly pulled my .45 in case he wanted to try something.

"Chill," he said and threw his hands up.

"Nah, just move out my way, Tonka," I told him.

"I will, but tell me you still love me." He looked at me with tears in his eyes.

I hated when he did this shit because I always broke down for him, but I couldn't do it this time.

"Call a cleanup crew, Tonka." I walked past him, and he grabbed me from behind.

"Baby, please. I swear I won't ever do this type of shit again. You my life, Queen." He squeezed me.

"No, Tonka, we done." I started crying as he tried to kiss me.

"You my queen, shawty, come on."

"Tonka, you gotta let me go."

I got tired of trying to get loose. He had to let me go physically and mentally.

"Okay, can I just fuck you one more time?" He started to run his hands up my legs, and I felt disgusted.

"You really ain't gon' get wet for me?" he asked.

"Nigga, you got dead bodies to be worried about. I got a son to live for, and what we got is only killing me, Tonka. Just be a good father," I said, and that made him release me.

"Go. Get the fuck out then, bitch." Feeling free, I grabbed my bags and went downstairs then walked right out the door.

I knew this was the start of my new life, or so I thought. But, again, the streets had a funny way of saying that ain't no love to be shown, no matter who you are.

A few weeks later, I sat in my new house, making lunch for Tadius after we got back from his little league game.

I heard knocking at the door, and I thought it was Tonka coming late to say he was sorry that he missed Tadius' little league game.

"Mommy, the door," Tadius called out.

He was looking at cartoons in the living room when I came out of the kitchen.

"Who is it?" I looked out the peephole and saw this nigga standing there who I had never seen before.

"I need to talk to you about Tonka," he said.

"I ain't got shit to do with him. How the fuck you know where I live?" I said.

"Bitch, that nigga told me he gave you something of mine," he said and kicked my door.

"I don't know what the fuck you talkin' 'bout!"

I went and grabbed my piece from the top of the coat closet.

"Open the fuckin' door and gimme my dope and my money!" He kicked the door.

I knew I had to kill this nigga before he got in there. Just as I was about to shoot through the door, he stopped kicking. I waited a minute before I looked out the peephole, and I felt relieved he wasn't there anymore.

"The hell."

Tadius was curled up on the couch, looking scared.

"It's okay, man."

I started to walk toward him, and then I felt pain in my leg after a bang, and I realized gunshots were sounding, and I had been hit. Bullets were flying through the window.

I hit the floor and crawled over to Tadius just as the bullets stopped.

"Baby, I got you."

I looked out the window before standing with Tadius in my arms. His body was limp, and I realized he had blood on his neck.

"Tadius?" I leaned him back and saw a bullet hole through his forehead.

"AHHHHHHHHH AHHHHHHHHHHH NOOOOOOOOO!!!!!!! MY BAAAABBBYYYYY!!" I screamed until I blacked out and had to be awakened by the police and EMTs.

***

It took me until this funeral to even come to grips with the fact that my son had been murdered, and it took even longer to come to grips with the fact that Tonka was the reason that nigga was at our house. I was about to get in the limo from the burial when Base came up to me.

"I'm so sorry about what happened, Queen." He held my hand, and I pulled it back.

"Where he at, Base?" I asked him with my voice quivering.

"I don't know, but everybody been looking for him. That was some real foul shit he pulled on you. He robbed that nigga Jake and told him you had his shit then ran off. That shit ain't right," he said.

"You right, it ain't. I'm gon' kill him about my son. I should have done it a long time ago. Don't ever come around me again, Base. You affiliated with that nigga, so you guilty by association." I got in, and the limo pulled away.

I buried my heart that day and hadn't let anyone come near me since.

I found Jake, the nigga who killed my son, but I didn't kill him right away. Instead, I killed every adult in his immediate family. I killed his barber, I killed people who owed him money, I killed everybody but the kids. I didn't have that in me.

When I finally felt satisfied that he understood I wasn't going to stop, I put his own dick in his mouth and watched him bleed out in front of me as his daughter watched, then I killed her mother and left her at the train station.

Tonka never showed back up, but I would never stop looking for his ass for as long as I breathed. For now, I was out here on my own.

Two years later

Sitting on the crate and looking at the last five vials that I had in my hand, I shook them around, just out of sheer boredom. I thought about how I had to grab that money from the stores for the lottery scam that we had going on. When it came to a hustle, I was always smart. I always saw people scanning their scratch-offs and shit, then they would throw the shit in the box on the floor when it said no winner. What we did was rig the machines, and every scratch ticket came up a loser. We could collect the boxes at the end of the night and scan them at working machines and cash out. Shit, we got a twenty thousand dollar one a few times. That's what kept my bricks rolling in. That extra money we got made us good.

"Aye, sis, we need some more work. This shit goin' too fast," Parquita ran up and said. I had her working for me now, and we made good money.

I ended up getting a few blocks off the strength of me being Tonka's old girl. I still had a few friends that I made through him, and I used that to my advantage.

"Damn, y'all killin' it," I said and gave her my last five. "We might as well wrap this shit up for the night," I told her.

"Aight, meet me at the car." She nodded.

Parquita had turned into a stud over time. She used to be girly and shit, but she changed one day, and she had bitches lined up for her. It was crazy.

"Aye, shorty, you got another cig?" I heard a male voice ask.

"Nah." I pushed my pack into my pocket before lighting it up.

"Bitch, I saw the pack," he said, and I turned my lip up.

"Who the fuck—"

Click.

I heard the familiar sound and turned around and saw some young nigga with his gun on me.

"You a bold as lil' nigga." I continued to smoke.

"Run that money, Queen," he said, and some other lil dude came out the cut, holding his gun, but he was shaking. He was the weak link.

"You wanna die for a few thousand?" I asked the scary one.

"Man, shut the fuck up and run that shit." The more dominant one walked up and went in my pocket.

I saw Parquita setting up behind a car with Crystal, one of my other runners, then I peeped Viloria get closer behind another car.

The niggas ran off after taking my money, but only because I let them.

I saw them both drop at the same time by the time they got to the end of the block without a fucking sound. I made sure we had silencers on every piece we carried.

"Damn." I shook my head and took another drag.

"You still wild, I see," I heard Base's voice.

I turned around and saw him standing there looking the fuck good. He had changed over the last two years, but I did remember telling him to stay the fuck away from me.

"Why you here?" I asked defensively.

"I wanted to see how you was, and I see you doin' your thing." He pointed to the niggas' bodies being dragged off the curb.

"Yeah, well." I shrugged. He brought back painful memories; he was a reminder of Tonka.

"Oh shit!" I heard a nigga say as he ran off from where they were dragging the bodies.

"His bitch ass finna call the police." I shook my head.

"Look, Queen, I know you lost a lot, baby girl, but I was always on your side. It killed me that you didn't want me to even try to comfort you, ma. I always figured you would leave him alone, and I would have my shot," he said, and I was a little shocked that he admitted that.

"Well, I guess we won't ever know."

"Why not?" he asked.

"Base..."

"Queen," he shot right back.

I heard the police nearing, and I knew we had to get the fuck.

"Take a ride with me." Base grabbed my arm as I saw my girls pulling up.

I waved them on and got in the car with Base.

"You look good, girl, even for a lil' dope girl." He laughed as we cruised.

"Thank you. I see you kept yourself up."

"I have, but let's get back to you. How much you movin' out here?" he asked.

"Why?"

"Because I asked," he said with this deep ass bass.

"A few kilos a week."

"I see you got some good corners too. You don't need to be out there alone, though, Queen. Let me get your back and put you on," he said.

"I'm already on, Base."

"Not like I can put you on. You need a nigga to take care of you out here, girl."

"We take care of ourselves."

"Not them, you." He looked at me, and I shook my head no.

"I'm cool on niggas, Base. I just don't have time for that shit right now."

"Yeah, right now, but once I spit my game, shawty, you finna be on it." He smiled, and I couldn't help but laugh.

"Nigga, you really comin' at me? I ain't never think you saw me that way," I said, thinking of how he was always so nice and shit.

"Well, that's the problem. You told a nigga to step, and I did, but I came back cuz I had to. I couldn't let the chance of a yeah or no haunt a nigga. So, what's up? You finna let me be what you need?" he asked.

I still declined, but I gave him my number, and we began to chat and shit.

He kept his promise of getting me more weight, and he even sent protection. We never got robbed or nothing. I asked around and found out he came all the way up to Boss level, working under some big time nigga from Italy, who was half black. I was happy for him.

After a few months of just talking, I let him take me out on a date.

Our first date was a show on South beach. Trina and French Montana were performing, and since I liked them both, I was good. When I saw how Base pulled out all the stops and went hard, I was feeling it. We had the VIP, where we chilled with both of them and got to go on stage and all.

"Man, that shit was dope." I fixed my white leather jacket and adjusted the matching mini skirt.

"Why you fidgeting? You look good, Queen." Base stopped at this nigga selling white and red roses. "Mix them up," he told him. "That shit set your outfit off," he said as he handed me the bundle.

"Thanks." I blushed.

"I'ma tear down that hard exterior," he said.

"Nah, this shit here to stay," I assured him.

"It ain't gotta be." He pulled me to him and kissed me so emotionally that I pulled back.

"Base, you don't have to lie to me." I smiled slightly.

"I'm not lyin' about shit." He looked offended.

"I know what you want. You wanna fuck me, possess me, and run game. I ain't stupid." I pointed to my head.

"No, I wanna fuck you, love you, and keep you safe." He ran his own list.

"Damn, I want me a nigga to do all that shit for me." This drunk bitch walked past and gave Base the fuck me eyes.

"He did me dirty, Base. You know he did." I turned around so he wouldn't see me cry.

"I know, Queen. Let me heal you, baby. You can't spend your life hurt behind him, boo." He wrapped his arms around me, and I gave in and hugged him back.

"Take me home," I told him.

He kissed me and nodded.

When we got to my house, I was barbaric. I hadn't had dick in seven months, and I thought I was okay until now.

"Damn." My eyes rolled when he began to bite and suck on my neck.

"You got some pretty ass titties." He ripped my bra straight off my body and massaged my titties.

My pussy was getting so wet as I started to ache for the dick.

"Finna eat this lil shit." He moved my thong to the side and sucked on my pussy like a Jolly Rancher.

This nigga was nasty as fuck with it too. Where had this head been all my life? He gripped and massaged my thighs, making noises like he was eating some good ass food.

"Oh shit." I jumped when I felt his thumb in my ass.

It didn't take any time after that for me to cum all over his damn face like a madwoman. This nigga was skilled, and he knew it.

"You almost broke my neck." He climbed between my legs, then pulled a tissue out the box on my nightstand and wiped his face.

"We need a condom." I went to grab one from the drawer when he grabbed one out of his jeans on the floor.

"We gotta hit the clinic, so I can hit it raw," he said and kissed me.

"How you know it's gon' happen again?" I saw him rolled the condom over his big ass dick and knew I was full of shit.

"Exactly."

He saw my lust and pushed his dick into me. I latched onto him when he hit my back wall.

"I told you, shorty, I got everything you need." He started to stroke deep into a bitch's soul.

"Pussy silky as fuck," he grunted, in this deep, sexy, satisfied voice that gave me chills.

"Nigga, you gon' make me cum, talkin' like that."

I arched my back, and he wrapped his arms through the space and hit me with hard strokes until I started to cum.

Base pulled out and stood up on the side of the bed then turned me over. He licked my pussy while my ass was up in the air, but he stopped and pushed his dick back in me then continued his assault on my pussy until I tried to tap out on him. He had so much more in him that he gave me two consistent hours of dick, and I was dead by the time he came.

"Man, I won't be able to walk." I was laid out breathless.

"Good, then you can stay right here and let me give you some more."

"Hell nah. Not for a few days." I laughed.

"You was everything I thought, though," he said as he kissed the back of my neck.

I had to admit that nigga was king ding-a-ling.

"Now what?" I asked as I watched the tree out the window move from the wind.

"You give me my shot." He kissed me deeply, and I felt his dick getting hard again.

"You popped a bean, nigga?" I asked, ready to run for my life.

"Nope. I just know quality pussy." He wrapped his arm around me from the side and slid his dick back into me but raw this time.

"Nigga!" I started to protest, but when I felt them strokes again, I just took it and made sure to drag his ass to the clinic in the morning.

***

Of course, y'all know we ended up together. I had to admit I was wrong about him, but I still couldn't love him the way I was supposed to. Even after a year and a half of us being together, I couldn't feel like I wanted to let my guard down. That caused a lot of stress for us at first, but he kind of took his time with me, and I appreciated that shit. I had strong feelings for him, and I felt like that shit should count for something.

We still lived separately, and I didn't want it any other way right now. I wanted my own shit, and he could have his as long as we respected and trusted each other. I never wanted to feel like I had to depend on a nigga again, and he understood that too. So, instead, we just spent the night at each other's place every night, but we still had the option of our own space when we needed it.

"You wanna go to this lil' barbecue my cousin is having this weekend?" Base asked me as we sat on the bed after he gave me that daddy dick.

"Yeah, that's cool. I ain't got shit to do," I said as I looked at my phone.

"You get that new shipment? I told Sosa pussy ass to give you them extra bricks for that short shit they pulled last time."

"Hell yeah, and he gave me five extra. I thought I was gon' have to smoke his punk ass." I laughed.

"Nah, I can't let you take my nigga out. We been ridin' a long ass time." He kissed my thigh, and I felt that electricity he always sent through my body.

"Your sweat smells good," he said and licked me.

I giggled and handed him the blunt.

"You nasty." I watched him get up and admired his sexy ass body.

"Oh, did I tell you how that dude, Paco, came through and tried to get stupid with us the other day?" I said.

"What? You already handled him?" He turned to me.

He hated to hear a nigga disrespected me out here.

"Nah, we let him breathe, bae. He was high as fuck, and that was his first offense."

I got up, and he watched my titties bounce. I could feel my twenty-one-inch bundles touching my bare ass.

"Nah, fuck that. Sometimes niggas get a pass and come back like shit sweet." He went to the bathroom and turned the shower on.

"You right, boo."

I kissed him, and he pulled me close then looked into my eyes.

"You thought about what I asked you?" he said, and I turned away.

"I'm not ready," I said, and he looked disappointed.

"Come on, I been patient, but I want certain things too, Queen," he said, speaking on having a baby. We had discussed it.

"I know, but we not even living together and stuff."

"So, when you gon' be ready to live together? You said you wanted your own place, so I respected that shit."

"Base, please, not right now. You know I still grieve for Tadius, and I feel guilty about having another baby. It's like replacing him." I looked at the picture that I kept on the dresser.

"It's called living, Queen."

I shut down like I always did when the subject came up.

"Aight, man." He jumped in the shower, and I closed the door.

I knew I was wrong, but I felt like I should at least have my shit together and be able to even love him like he deserved before we added a baby.

When he got out, he went to the closet that I made for him.

"So, you mad at me now?" I asked Base as he put on his deodorant.

"Nah." He slammed it on the dresser.

"Okay, look, you know I don't like when we fight." I walked up to him, and he looked down at me.

"I ain't fightin' you, shorty." He put his hands up.

"I mean here." I touched his heart.

"You fightin' me, Queen. I want the whole thing wit' chu. I know you got trust issues, but we gettin' close to two years. Sum gotta shift."

"Okay, so what you sayin'? You gonna go find a bitch to get pregnant because I ain't ready?" I asked with my hands on my hips.

"I would never do you foul like that. Man, look, just keep your wall up, and next thing you know, it's finna be five years, and we on the same shit." He put his shirt and chain on.

"I'ma holla at chu later." He kissed me and left.

I always felt like the bad guy no matter what, and now was no exception. All he wanted was a wife, and all I wanted to do was protect myself.

I called Parquita to see what she was getting into tonight.

"Damn, you know how to fuck a bitch shit up," she said when she picked up, and I laughed.

Parquita said I had the worst timing when it came to phone calls because she would be with a bitch about to fuck, and I would call.

"My bad. Tell shorty she a be aight." I laughed.

"Nah, I'ma have to call you back, sis, cuz you ain't lookin' at what I'm lookin' at." She hung up, and I shook my head with a smile.

I sat in the house now, wishing I would have made up with Tonka before he left. I hated when he was in the streets, and we were mad at each other. Maybe it was time for me to compromise on something. He gave me everything I wanted, yet I can't give him something.

I ended up swallowing my pride and calling him.

"Wassup, baby?" he said when he picked up, and I melted inside. I loved how he still called me baby even when he was pissed.

"I'm sorry," I said, and the line went silent. "You hear me?" I asked.

"Yeah, I'm just tryna process the fact that you saying it." He laughed.

"Oh, shut up, nigga. I love you," I told him.

"I love you too, girl. Look, won't you get dressed and meet me at the trap in a few hours."

"Okay. And maybe us moving in together ain't so bad," I said.

"I'm glad you said it cuz I thought I was finna have to kidnap your ass and hold you hostage every night."

"Damn, nigga... for real?" I laughed as I looked for something to wear.

"Gimme three hours, shawty, and come holla at cha nigga."

"Aight."

I hung up and put on his favorite outfit, which was a V neck that dipped to my navel and a pair of jean shorts up my ass with some cheek exposed. I was gonna fuck the shit out of him tonight, and in this, it wouldn't take long to rock his dick up.

I did my make up and put the top of my hair up in a genie ponytail, letting the back hang.

"Okay, bitch." I slid on my black vest and looked in the mirror.

I sat and smoked, watched some TV, and talked shit to my cousin Trisha on the phone. I got this eerie feeling and decided to just leave and be with Base.

My phone began to ring as I left, and it was Aunt Bella.

"Hey, Auntie," I said when I picked up.

"Hey, I just wanted to be the first to tell you. Ya mama home."

I felt overcome with emotion and realized why I had that feeling.

"Wow. Where is she?"

"She in a halfway house. We should take her out this weekend. She been in there a long ass time, Queen."

"I know. I'll get something planned for her," I said.

"Now you try real hard to build a new relationship, Queen. She needs her daughter." She hung up, and I felt more nervous than anything. After that last visit, I just couldn't face her, knowing that she knew I put her there. After all her suffering with my father, I put the nail in the rest of her youthful coffin.

When I got to the trap, I saw my baby sitting out front smoking on a blunt and talking to some niggas. I got out, and he touched his chest, then tossed his head back.

"You know what these shorts do to me, Ma," he said and pulled me onto his lap.

His workers walked into the building and left us alone.

"You gon' get niggas killed walking around like that." He bit his lip and grabbed my ass as he held me in his lap. "So, you serious about us livin' together?"

He looked into my eyes, and I felt some of the doubt I carried vanish.

"Yours or mine? Because I like my place better." I kissed him, and he pulled back.

"Next, we finna have our son." He touched my stomach, and I lay on his shoulder.

"Your determination is real." I laughed, and we slowly kissed.

"Let's go hit the water. We can go to the beach and make mufuckas jealous." He stood up and placed me on my feet.

"Let's go, nigga." I liked walking in front of him because he liked to see my ass move.

We go to his car, and I smiled. I loved how sexy his whip was, and it was sexier how he drove it.

"Let me get it." He opened the passenger door.

"I want a Brazilian steak, baby." He tapped my exposed ass cheek and stopped abruptly after hearing a car backfire.

"Get down." He jumped on top of me, knocking me to the floor.

I hear more loud booms and realized it was gunshots.

"Stay down, shawty," Base said with a grunt.

"Shit, you hit, baby." I was able to turn around and see that he was bleeding and in pain.

"Get the fuck outta here, baby," he said with shallow breathing.

"No! We gonna get you to the hospital." I could see some of his people shooting at whoever was shooting at us.

"Queen. Let me take care of you. Leave."

He went into his pocket and gave me his key. Since the passenger door was open, I tried to pull him in, but he let me go and pulled his gun.

"Queen, go, get the fuck outta here, baby. Ima see you at home," he said and kissed me.

He was hurt badly, and I knew I wouldn't see him at home.

"Base, please get in," I cried, trying to pull on him, but he pulled back.

"I love your ass, girl. Go!" he said.

He slid behind my car, and I pulled off as the bullets started to hit his car.

"Fuck."

I drove off, and when I saw Base lying down and shooting, I couldn't do it. I couldn't leave him. If it was time for me to be with my son, then so be it. I missed him anyway.

I kicked my shoes off, jumped out of the car, and opened the trunk. I went in the spare, where I knew he kept an automatic in all his vehicles.

I picked it up and loaded the clip. Taking a deep breath, I walked into the war zone.

"Lord, forgive me of my sins. If I die, let me go to heaven and be with my son and my brother. Amen," I prayed before shooting at the black Lincoln Town Car that was shooting in Base's direction.

I felt the sting in my arm and realized I was hit.

I looked to the left and saw a ghost, which caused me to freeze. Thinking quickly, I shot downward at his legs because ain't no way I would let him die without hearing me.

I watched Tonka fall to the ground and try to slide toward an Impala that was waiting for him.

The Lincoln hadn't moved, and I saw that no more bullets were flying from that car, so I was ready to take whoever was driving the Impala, but they sped away.

I held my arm and ran over to Tonka.

"You got our son killed, MUHFUCKA!" My hands shook. I couldn't even feel my wound anymore because my anger had taken over.

"I didn't do shit!" He tried to quickly raise his gun, and I shot him three more times in the gut.

He dropped the gun, but this roach still lived.

"Why you send that nigga to kill us, huh?" I screamed.

He was going in and out.

"You went and fucked Base, though? Y'all some scandalous ass mufuckas." He coughed up blood.

"That's what the fuck you worried about? Who I was fucking when I told you our son is dead, nigga?" I stomped him in the face with the heel of my foot.

I started to walk away, knowing he would die soon. I needed to get to Base.

"I killed TJ too, bitch!" he spat.

I turned around and watched him smile then start to laugh.

"Yeah, then I thought about how funny it was to be fucking his sister. You were so in love with the nigga who killed—"

I walked up and emptied the clip in his face as I heard sirens.

"Shit."

I ran over when I saw Base's people carrying him to a truck. I jumped in and laid his head in my lap.

"Didn't I tell you to go home, ma?" he asked in a somber tone that shook me to my soul. He was dying; he was leaving me like everybody I ever loved. "I love you, Queen." I saw a tear fall from his eye, and I touched my nose to his.

"I love you too, Base," I cried as we drove, and I heard his last breath in my ear.

I was dangerous. Anything I loved died, and I realized I was meant to be alone. I couldn't love, or I would lose them, and it wasn't fair to anyone, so I chose a life of solitude and money.

I found Base's plug, Marsel. Well, actually, he found me. He heard about how I stood tall for Base that night, and he floated me some bricks. Now, here I am, five years later, sitting on top of the drug world. I had to kill a lot of niggas and sell a lot of work to get to where I am now. Niggas tried me, of course, because I was a female, but I always showed them this pussy ain't shit but decoration. I was savage first, and that's how I came to be who I am.

So, there I was, sitting in my den, looking out the window and shedding tears about my life and all the pain I suffered. Then, I quickly wiped them. I loved Wessie from afar, and my curse still reached his ass.

I needed to go and see what was up with him. I had met him years ago and fell in love from the first day we met at the beach. His family had an agreement with me, and his people broke it, so I fed them to the sharks and came to approach me about it. From first sight, he was my type, but I couldn't let that be known. The way he loved his family, his sisters especially, let me know that he would treat a girl right. I couldn't let him, though; I knew what would happen. He would die like everybody else.

I lost my aunt Bella last year, and I couldn't blame shit but cancer for that, but she definitely was one of the last people who had a piece of my heart. I didn't want death for Wessie, so I left him alone and hurt.

"I got the car out front," Tevony came back inside and said.

"I'm driving myself." I walked past her and went upstairs and saw Peace standing at the top of the stairs with her machine gun around her neck.

Of course, the head of security was Parquita. Yeah, she was still my homie, and we been at this shit a long time together. She was one of the few I fully trusted. That was hard for me, but she had earned that shit over time.

I went to the bathroom and got in my four-way shower then hit the rainforest setting. The walls lit up, and trees appeared. Birds began to fly, and rainforest sounds filled the space. I had this shower specially made to look like I was wherever I wanted to be at the time. With all four walls, it really looked like I was showering in the rainforest.

After I got out, I picked a gold and white shorts two-piece and grabbed a pair of black seven-inch stilettos. I wondered if I should be extra with a mink stole or just let the blazer be. I went without the stole and put on a gold and diamond necklace. I tapped myself with House of Sillage and walked out of the room.

"Tevony, what you hear?" I asked.

"He in surgery, and um... his wife just got there," she said.

"Wife?" I looked at her like she was crazy.

"Yeah. Apparently, he's been married for three weeks."

"To who?"

She shook her head, and I leaned my head to the side.

"Sonovia Stanfield," she said, and I instantly became furious.

"I know you lyin', Tevony," I said, not believing this nigga was married and who he was married to.

Marsel told me his daughter got married, but I just didn't know who the unlucky bastard was. Had I accepted Marsel's invitation to the wedding, I would have known and gagged.

The Stanfield brothers, Sonovia's brothers, were my sworn enemies ever since they killed one of my corner boys, and I had to kill five of theirs. The only reason I haven't wiped them completely out was because of their father and who he happened to be. My fucking connect turned business partner! Marsel. He understood his kids were stupid ass motherfuckers, and his daughter had a mouth that she couldn't back up.

The crazy part is, I didn't know why the fuck she had issues with me. I didn't even know they had a daughter. He didn't even have family pictures in his house; he said he kept them in his home in Italy because he didn't want his memories to die here if he did. But, anyway, I had met her the year after I got on with Marsel on the business end. She had been out of the country for a few years after some tragedy she suffered. He begged me for a truce, and I gave him one because he had been good to me over the years.

"Wessie really knows how to pick 'em." I walked past Tevony and went into my garage.

After surveying all the cars, I chose to drive the Bentayga. I always loved Bentleys, and this was by far my favorite.

When I got inside, I turned on some old school Lil Kim and pulled off.

"I used to be scared of the dick, now I throw lips at the shit, handle it like a real bitch." I rapped along as I took one of my clover cigarettes out the box and lit it.

I couldn't believe this nigga Wessie was really married to this bitch, Sonovia. How the fuck the people I had watching him didn't see it? How could I be mad, though? I was the one who left him.

When I got to the hospital, I saw Wessie's sister, Princess, standing outside with two children running around her.

I pulled up right beside her, and she looked at my car suspiciously until I got out.

"Queen, is that you?" She covered her mouth, and we hugged.

"You look good, girl," I said, admiring her Versace outfit. I had a similar one.

I always thought she and Delasia, his other sister, were beautiful.

"I'm glad you came to see him. He'll be happy about that," she said.

"Well, I hear he got married, so I don't know how his wife will feel about it. We got history," I told her.

"I can't stand her Queen. I mean, I wish you two would have worked it out because this bitch works my last nerve." Princess shook her head.

"Trust me, I know the feeling. You going up?" I asked, and she nodded.

"I see you got you some kids," I said.

"Yup, they bad as hell."

I looked at the cute boy and girl.

"So, how's everything going with you?" I asked.

"Good. Priest is still my baaaby. I opened another rink," she said.

I nodded. "Well, let me know how I can donate. Take my number."

"That'll work," she said, and we exchanged numbers.

"Sis!" Delasia ran up, and she jumped up and down when she saw me. "The Queen herself. Looking the fuck good as usual." She hugged me.

"You always so animated," I said as I hugged her back.

"I missed you. Ugh, did you tell her about—"

"Girl, yes," Princess cut her off and rolled her eyes as well.

"I swear, Queen, this hoe is unreal." Delasia shook her head.

"I know," I replied as we approached the room.

When I walked in, I saw Sonovia sitting next to Wessie, who was either sleeping or induced.

"Queen, what the hell are you doin' here?" Sonovia asked.

"Queen?" the nurse asked me.

I looked at her like, *who the fuck are you?*

"Yeah?" I cocked my head.

"He's been saying your name since they put him under before surgery," she replied, and I smiled.

"He has not. This ain't your job, is it?" Sonovia spat.

"Lil' girl, I don't work for you. Find somebody else mama to play with 'fore my daughters be on your ass," the nurse said and walked out.

I wanted to high five her old ass.

"You didn't answer my question." Sonovia looked back at me.

"That's because I would never answer to the likes of you." I walked up to Wessie's side and looked down at his gorgeous face. He still had his bull ring. Only his ass could pull that off and still be a thug with his shit.

"How you know Queen?" Delasia asked Sonovia.

"Why y'all think she picked him?" I looked at Princess and Delasia. "She knew what he meant to me." I mugged Sonovia.

"Bitch, please. Everything ain't about you, Queen. I know in your little world that's hard to conceive." Sonovia got up.

"What you doin' here?"

I heard Wessie speak, and I froze.

I turned around and looked at him, fighting back my tears. Happy that he was breathing and okay.

"I just... I had to see if you was okay." I looked at him.

"The last time I heard from you, you killed our baby," he said like he still hated me for that.

"Wait, what?" Sonovia spoke up.

"Come with us. They need a minute," Princess said.

"This my husband. I ain't going a damn place," Sonovia said.

"Sonovia, now you know I act a fool wherever," I warned her.

"Yeah, and let my father cut your shit off."

"Bitch, you speakin' business in public." I was ready to say fuck the truce.

"Aye, Sonovia, go 'head out," Wessie told her.

She pointed at me and walked out.

Once Wessie and I were alone, he stared at me for a minute.

"So, what's up, Queen?" he asked me, and I shrugged.

"Nothin'. I just had to make sure—"

"Make sure of what? You ain't gave a fuck for a long time. Why you care now?"

"Who said I didn't care? I just wanted you to be happy, Wessie," I said.

"Bein' with you would have made me happy. You havin' my baby would have made me fuckin' happy! Not you telling me you can't for no fuckin' reason." He was still hurt.

"You know how I felt, Wessie." I looked down, ashamed to even look at him.

"I thought I did."

"I still feel like that." I ignored his last comment.

"Good. I moved the fuck on, Queen, so you can let that guilt go. Play with somebody else, shawty." He looked past me.

"I'm glad you okay, Wessie."

I put on my shades and held my head up as I walked out.

"You okay?" I heard Princess ask.

I nodded. "Call me."

As soon as I got on the elevator, I burst into tears.

"I was scared, Wessie," I said aloud as the elevator doors opened.

I saw Priest and Vibe, Princess and Delasia's husbands about to get on.

"Shit, Queen. Shawty, wuz good?" Vibe spoke first.

"Ain't shit. Look at you two, still fine as hell." I laughed.

"You know?" Priest rubbed his face.

"It's nice seeing y'all, though. If you here a few days, I'll send Princess my addy, and we can get together," I told them and walked out of the hospital.

I had a text from Presia.

Presia: *Can I come over?*

Me: *Yeah, be naked too.*

Wessie Rain

"Wessie, you knew the beef I had with Queen. I told you about her, yet you remained silent." Sonovia paced around the bedroom, irritating the fuck outta me.

It had been a week since the hospital, and every day, she found a way to bring up Queen.

"Aye, Sonovia. Like, for real, shut the fuck up. I got shot, bitch, and you sittin' here speakin' on some old shit? Man, fuck." I picked up my phone and almost set a jet to hit Oakland and fuck with my people.

"Damn, I gotta be a bitch?" She smacked my phone out of my hand.

"See." I ran my hand over my mouth and chuckled because I was mad and didn't wanna hurt her.

"You know what, I shouldn't have married your ass," she said, and I nodded.

"Shit, I agree. You showed who the fuck you really are after you got that ring, shawty." I got up, holding my stomach, still in pain.

"Wow, all because I ask you a fuckin' question?" She stormed out of the room, and I was glad she shut the fuck up.

Sonovia was cool as fuck when we first met. She was that sweetheart type and shit, or at least she pretended to be. After a while, I realized she was spoiled as fuck, but she had good pussy, and I had feelings for her and shit, so I kept fucking with her. But it seemed like since the wedding, she had been on bullshit and blowing my life. Her father was a cool ass dude, but her brothers, Toreese and Malcom, were a different story. I didn't vibe with their ass, and I only came across them when Queen and I were fucking around, and she put me on with her plug.

"Look, Wessie, I don't wanna fight." Sonovia came back into the room.

"You always say that shit right before you start a fuckin' argument."

"I fuckin' hate you." She left back out, and I guarantee she would be back five more times.

I got myself dressed and was hurt as a bitch, but I couldn't stay there with her.

I grabbed my keys, and when I got downstairs, she was on the phone, crying and shit.

"He acts like he hates me now," she cried into the phone.

I sighed and left the house. I ain't have time for that shit right now when a nigga was tryna recover and shit.

When I got to the car, she opened the front door and tried to run out, but I sped around the circle driveway and got the fuck outta there.

I called my homie Sidwell. We called him Sid, though. That shit was too much to say.

"Wassup, nigga? How you feelin'?" he asked me.

"Shid, I'm good. I had to get the fuck out of the house. Shawty in there on some goofy shit."

"Man, that's your wife. Thick and thin, nigga." He chuckled.

Sid ain't believe in marriage. He always thought it was like limiting your life. He just ain't find that one yet. Shit, obviously, I didn't either because I didn't think it was supposed to be like this.

"Won't you fall through? Tay and them finna come through and jump on the sticks," he said excitedly.

"Aight, I'm on the way," I said and hung up.

I called my cousin Jacca to see if he wanted to come and chill too. He had just moved there and didn't really know any niggas.

"Wassup, blood?" he said in his country ass accent. He was from Mississippi.

"Ain't shit. You wanna roll through my folks' house wit me?"

"Yeah, that's cool. Can I bring this lil' bitty I met?"

"Bitty? Uh, aight, whatever the fuck that means."

"Nigga, you know what I mean. Send me the spot, and I'll be there." He hung up, and I kept driving until I got to Sid's house.

"Wassup, how them wounds?" Sid opened the door when I got to the porch.

"They aight, my nigga. My cousin finna come over too."

"That's cool. Man, that nigga needs to get his mama to send some more of them sweet potato pies and strawberry cakes. I would have been a fat nigga livin' with her." He touched his stomach.

"Man, she be cookin' like a mufucka. I said I was goin' there for Thanksgiving." I walked in and saw some of our friends already on the game.

"Wassup, Wessie? I'm surprised the wife let you out." Tay laughed.

"Nigga, you mad you can only get bitches who want you to give 'em the neck," I shot back, and niggas fell out laughing.

"Man, fuck you, nigga." He put his middle finger up.

"Aye, you need to talk to Quincy punk ass too." Sid pointed at me.

"For what, nigga?" I asked.

"He did it again. He dropped the shit off at the wrong address, and the truck got towed," he said.

"Nigga, I know the fuck you ain't tellin' me that nigga lost our work?" I looked around at them, wondering why the fuck they were playin' video games and shit.

"Yeah, but we got it back and sent it to Ice," he said.

"Man, that was Ice's shit?" I asked.

"Yeah, it was a few bricks missin', bruh. He was understanding, though," Yella said.

"Nigga, understanding? Y'all niggas let this dude rob us and call it a mistake?" I laughed.

"Come on. Put that shit down," I told them.

Yeah, they were my niggas, but they also were my lieutenants and worked for me.

"You should have just dropped his ass, nigga." I saw everybody put the controllers down.

"Nigga, we got one quarter left." Mick motioned to the TV.

"I don't give a fuck." I walked out and saw my cousin pull up in his 64.

"Damn, I missed it already?" Jacca asked and opened the passenger side.

"The fuck?" I watched this chick, Angel, who I used to fuck with step out.

"Hey, Wessie." She waved.

"You know my cousin?" Jacca asked her.

"Yeah, we used to fuck back in Oakland."

Everybody looked shocked by her abrasive ass bullshit right in Jacca's face.

"You wild as shit. She prolly only got with chu to keep stalkin' me and shit." I looked at Angel, who had gained a little weight. She looked good, like AJ Johnson, when she did *House Party*.

"Nigga, everything ain't about you." She smacked her teeth.

"Then why you move to Miami?" I asked, and she looked dumbfounded.

"Exactly. Aye, my bad, Jacca. We got some shit to do." I slapped hands with him, and I could tell that Angel was in her feelings about the shit.

"Damn, now I wonder if she got me shot," I said to Sid, and he started laughing.

I had no idea who took a shot at me, but it could have been anybody. I don't start too much shit, but I finished it whenever it came to me. I had niggas still mad that I beat their teeth in right in front of their wife and kids. Shit, maybe it was one of them niggas. I wasn't even worried about finding out right now. Good shit comes to niggas who wait.

"That nigga stay in NW 66, right?" I asked Sid as I pulled off.

"Yup." He nodded.

We took the short drive since Sid only lived on NW 48th.

"So, what we finna do?" Sid asked, already pulling his gun from his waistband.

"I just wanna talk to the nigga." I got out and saw him sitting on the porch with his daughter.

"Aye, don't got damn shoot with that lil' girl on the porch," I told Sid.

"Nigga, I ain't that fucked up."

We walked up, and Quincy sat upright.

"Go 'head and keep playin' wit yo' kid, nigga. I ain't finna light you up yet," I told him.

"Laquisha!" Quincy called into the house.

This thick shorty came out wearing one of those half sweaters and a pair of booty shorts.

"Damn," I said as I stared at her.

"Ain't no need to be disrespectful," Quincy said.

I looked at Sid, and we both laughed as she took the little girl inside.

"Nigga, I'll fuck that bitch, and she a let me." I slapped hands with Sid.

"Look, I told Sid I was sorry about the shit. I keep fuckin' up," Quincy said, having the nerve to act like we were bothering him or something.

"Tell me, nigga. Tell me how you got it in your mind that you think I would let you keep stealing my shit and pretend it was a mistake?" I sat next to him and looked at Tay, Yella, and Mick as they anticipated my next move.

"I ain't—"

"You ain't what? Steal Ice's shit?" I asked.

"Nah, I just... I mean..." The way he stuttered should have forced a bullet in him, but his bitch saw me, and I would hate to have to kill her fine ass too.

"So, who you work with at the tow truck place?" I asked him, and he looked at me like he was caught.

"My cousin, Carlo." He put his hand over his face.

"Okay, cool. We finna go kill his ass, and you can sit here for a minute and think about what you did. Then, we comin' back for your ass when you good and scared," I said and jumped up.

"Come on, Wessie, bro," he pleaded.

"I'M NOT YOUR FUCKIN' BROTHER, NIGGA!" I pulled my gun and shoved it in his mouth.

He started to cry real tears.

"Man the fuck up, nigga!" I said, looking at him in disgust.

"What the fuck you doin'?" His bitch came back outside.

"Get the fuck back in the house." Sid kicked the door, and she jumped back and ran.

"Go enjoy your family, nigga." I hit him the back of the head, and we stepped off the porch.

"We should have killed his pussy ass right then and there," Sid said.

"I know, but we good. Come back tonight," I told him, and he nodded.

I didn't tolerate any type of stealing. A fuck up once, but two times and your life is expired in my eyes.

***

"Tell my nephew, happy birthday. Ima send him some good shit," I told Princess as I looked in Walmart to get those tiki lights for the backyard.

I was having a party to celebrate me opening my 6th luxury detail shop. I was trying to keep as much clean money as possible; I wasn't no clown ass dude who wouldn't have shit to show for my time in the street.

"Aye!" I called out to an employee who walked by.

She backtracked and came up to me.

"I need tiki lights," I told her.

"I told you to go in the garden section, dumb ass," Princess said on the phone, and I hung up.

"Garden center," the girl said, and I started laughing because Princess was right.

"You good now?" she asked.

"Yeah, I'm good." I realized how cute she was but remembered I was married. Damn.

I walked away from her and went to get them, and then I went and got my nephew some toys and shit. A whole cart full. I would have to pay out the ass to ship all this shit. After I paid for my stuff, I left and went home to see if the butcher had dropped off all the meat I ordered. I got over two thousand dollars' worth of different steak cuts, chicken, links, and seafood. All premium shit. I hired one of the top Pitmasters in Miami. He and his team would run the grills all night, and I had a soul food spot for the sides.

When I got home, I saw a black and yellow Camaro out front, and I gritted my teeth. It was Toreese, Sonovia's brother's car. I be two seconds from putting a bullet in his shit every time this nigga comes around.

"When I got out, I opened the trunk and walked all the tiki torches to the back then came in through the kitchen.

"I don't wanna have this party, to be honest," I heard Sonovia say.

"Then tell the nigga that this your shit too." I heard Toreese's punk ass.

"Then y'all both can get the fuck out. Who the fuck even invited you, nigga?" I looked at Toreese, and he turned his cap backward and shit like that was supposed to be scary.

"Nigga, this my sister's shit too. The fuck. She don't want a bunch of niggas running through her shit." He stood up.

"Y'all always gotta do this?" Sonovia said like she wasn't just about to talk shit to the nigga if I ain't step in.

"Nah, fuck that. Brother or not, this nigga can catch it." I looked at him and her.

"Try me," Toreese said, and I laughed.

"You ain't tough, nigga. You come from a tough nigga, but you soft. Don't play with guns, nigga, that's big boy shit." I looked at that little shit he had on his waist.

The doorbell chimed, and Sonovia ran to answer it.

"Wassup, nigga?" Sid walked in and slapped hands with me.

"Ain't shit. AT ALL," I said to him but looked at Toreese.

"Just go ahead, bro." Sonovia pushed him toward the door.

"Get your nigga in check," Toreese said as he closed the door.

"Boy, what?" I went to get at his ass when Sonovia jumped in my way.

"Nigga, what's up with that dude?" Sid asked.

"That dude is my brother. Don't be talkin' shit, Sid," Sonovia said and stormed off.

"Man, you got your work cut out." Sid shook his head.

"Them niggas gon' fuck around and find they asses in the ground. Keep talkin' slick." I walked to the backyard, and Sid helped me put all the decorations and shit up.

I started to miss my mother as I saw all the decorations. She loved parties. My life wasn't traditional at all. When my sister Princess and I were children, she was raped by two men, and our parents were murdered right in front of us. We got adopted by a white couple, and that's when Princess was added to our family. Alex, our adopted father, ended up being all three of our actual father, and that set all kinds of shit in motion. Anyway, our mother, Heather, killed herself after we found out she had something to do with Alex's death. The shit was fucked up all the way around. Still, I missed my family. I moved to Miami a few years ago, but my sisters still lived in San Francisco.

A few hours later, everything was in full swing, and the food was smelling right. I was hungry as hell, but I was too busy talking and shit to everybody.

"Aye, bro, your cousin just popped up with Angel wild ass," Sid came up and said.

"Man, this nigga must want some drama. She finna show her ass." I walked to meet them at the gate, but they were already in the backyard.

"Wassup, cuzzo." I dapped Jacca up.

"Man, that grill wassup right now. You can smell it down the street." He looked over my shoulder.

"Hey, Wessie." Angel pursed her lips.

"Sup." I raised my cup and drank down my E&J.

"Bae, you got the steak sauce, cuz people say the one on the table is empty." Sonovia walked up and ran her hand across my chest.

"Wassup, Sonovia?" Jacca hugged her.

"This you, Wessie?" Angel said, and I scoffed.

"I'm his wife." Sonovia showed her two-thousand-dollar ring.

"Oh, you married now, Wessie? That's wassup. Y'all got a nice house, girl," she said to Sonovia.

"Thank you, boo," Sonovia said in a fake voice.

"Let's grab some food." Jacca walked off with Angel.

"Who that?" Sonovia asked when they walked away.

"My cousin's girl," I told her.

"Then why she talkin' like she knows you?" Sonovia was getting loud, and I was getting impatient.

"What the fuck wrong wit' chu, man? You always mad about anything now. You pregnant or some shit?" I asked her, and she looked away.

"No, nigga, I just don't want you tryna dog me," she said with a sad ass look.

"I ain't tryna dog you. What the fuck changed about how I treat you, shorty? The only thing changin' is you."

I went to see if I put that box of A1 under the table. I had got the shit from BJ's so we wouldn't run out since I knew it would be so many people.

"Bro, we need that sauce," Tay said with two steaks and a ten-ounce lobster tail on his plate.

"I know. I think I left it in the house." I noticed the box wasn't there with the rest of the condiments.

I went inside and saw the box sitting on the floor next to the basement door. I went to grab it when I heard a noise downstairs.

"The fuck." I opened the door and went to see who the fuck was in my basement.

Grabbing my gun, I opened the basement door and went down the stairs.

Angel was coming out of the bathroom.

"It was one upstairs," I said with the gun on her.

"Damn, you gonna kill me for using the bathroom?" She threw her hands up.

"Don't let me find out you in here going through my shit," I said, and she smacked her teeth.

"Stop, Wessie, you treat me like you hate me," she said.

"You was on bullshit since you moved here. Now you with my cousin to try and get back close, but it ain't gon' work," I said through gritted teeth.

I was tired of playing with her ass at this point.

"I actually like Jacca. He knows how to handle pussy," she said.

"Okay, good for you. Go out back and piss in the bushes or whatever, but don't come back into my house," I told her.

She walked past me and turned around.

"Don't act like you don't miss this pussy, Wessie." She bent over and lifted her skirt, showing me that she didn't have no draws on.

"Wessie!" I heard Sonovia calling me.

This was just what the fuck I needed right now, for her to see us coming up the steps from the basement together.

"He down here!" Angel said loudly.

The door swung open, and Sonovia looked like she wanted to fly down the stairs.

"I knew it." She grabbed Angel's hair, and they started fighting on the landing. I went up and pulled them apart as Jacca walked in.

"What the fuck goin' on?" He grabbed Angel.

"They was down there fucking," Sonovia said.

"Damn, Wessie, I know you had her first, but you had to go behind my back and hit? You could have let me know first if you wanted to fuck her, damn," Jacca said.

"Wait, so you lied? You used to fuck with this bitch?" Sonovia said.

"I ain't fuck this bitch. She was down here, and I heard somebody. Why the fuck you think I got the gun?" I showed them.

"Why the fuck you lyin', Wessie?" Angel said, and I looked at her in disbelief.

"What going on?" Sid came in, followed by a few people.

"Fuck you, Wessie." Sonovia walked out, and I looked at Angel.

"Get this grimy bitch out my house," I told Jacca.

They walked out, and Sid came up.

"Nigga, what the fuck happened?" Sid asked.

"I don't know, but I paid too much for that food."

I grabbed the box of steak sauce then went out and ate. I knew I didn't do shit, and if Sonovia wanted to believe that bullshit, then cool, she could have it.

Sonovia Stanfield

"MMMMMMM, FUUUUUCK." I threw my head back and grinded harder on the dick.

"Damn." Jacca smacked my ass hard as he pushed into me, matching my rhythm.

"Don't cum yet," I warned him.

"I can't hold it." He tightened up, and I knew he had cum.

"Weak." I got up.

"Bitch, we been fuckin' for an hour. Weak these nuts." He got up with an attitude.

"I'm just sayin', I wasn't finished."

"I don't see how my cousin deal wit cho ass, shawty. Your pussy good, but your attitude makes me wanna fuck you up," Jacca said as he got his jeans.

"I'm sorry."

I looked at him, and I could tell he was still under my spell regardless of what he said. I had been putting this pussy on Jacca since his big, Jethro country ass hit the scene. Wessie was sexy and fine as hell, so it was no coincidence that his cousin was a big ole chocolate tree. I know it seems foul, but Wessie was just a pawn in a bigger chessboard. Yeah, I loved him, but I couldn't too hard.

When I saw that trash, Angel, I knew exactly who the bitch was. I knew everything about Wessie and his family plus anyone they ever came in contact with, and that was all research for Queen to get what she had coming to her ass.

"Come on. I need to lock my shit up." Jacca tried to rush me, and I looked at him like he was crazy.

"Nigga, I'm finna take my time. I can lock your door," I told him.

He shook his head and walked out of the room.

I liked Jacca, and he was a nice piece of dick, but too bad. If he could fuck with me after I kill his cousin, then cool. If not, he could go too.

After I heard Jacca leave, I grabbed my phone and called my brother Malcom.

"Yeah, mane." He picked up like he was irritated by me.

"Damn, what the fuck I do to you?" I asked.

"Nun, I'm busy. Wassup?"

Well, he was in a mood, so I decided to talk quickly.

"Did you find out what I asked you?"

"Yeah, She stayin' out in Opa locka," he said.

"Okay, thanks."

"Look, we got niggas you can go through for this. You doin' too much, lil sis," he said, and I simply hung up.

I didn't tell him how to handle his beefs, so he couldn't tell me shit about mine.

I grabbed my clothes and went to the bathroom to take a shower, so I could go and see my parents about this money. I had a trust fund set up ever since my father took over in the streets for my grandfather. I used a lot of that to have plastic surgery. For years, I went through depression after I lost the love of my life to a bitch who deserved to be where he is. I wasn't going to rest until she met that same fate.

When I got in my Maybach, I looked through my playlist and decided to fuck with Summer Walker. I jammed and smoked on half a blunt as I looked at the picture that I had hidden in my visor in case Wessie ever got into my car.

"Don't worry, baby, I'ma get her ass." I rubbed the picture with my thumb and wiped the tear that fell.

"We gonna get her," I repeated and closed the visor.

***

"I called your ass like six times, Wessie!" I yelled as he came in.

I hated that I actually had caught feelings for him because he was driving me crazy with the shit he pulled.

"I was busy." He looked at the food on the table.

"Yeah, well, I wanted to do something special, so I made dinner, thinking we could have some romance," I said, ready to cry.

I knew this was all for show, but like I said, I had caught feelings in the process, and this nigga was cold as fuck.

"We can still be romantic." He came around the table, and I tried not to smile.

"Don't hide that smile," he said.

I tried, but I couldn't help it.

"Ugh, why you gotta be like this?"

I got up and wrapped my arms around him. At times like this, I wished he didn't have to go, due to his choice in bitches. I knew how much Queen loved him, and soon, she would feel how I felt the night she took Tonka away from me.

"Qia, you need to do this shit for me."

Tonka was trying to convince me to help him set up this drug dealer, Jake, who lived across the street from me.

He always tried to flirt with me and shit, and when that nigga Tonka tried to play me for Queen, I fucked Jake, and good. I gave it to him on the regular until shortly after Queen and Tonka became official. He started to fuck with me again while they were together, basically their whole fake ass relationship. I could tell he was in love with her, but he must have loved me more because he was still fucking me and taking care of me.

"Okay, but if he finds out, I'm dead," I told Tonka.

"Man, fuck all that. I hear he got a safe full of dope and money. I need that shit." He looked at me and pulled on his blunt.

"So, what we gotta do?" I asked. "I want half."

"Aight, cool. Whatever, man, just go wash your pussy and knock on the door." He got up.

"Ain't shit wrong with my pussy, nigga," I said defensively.

"Yeah, well, wash it anyway." He made a call, and it seemed like he put the plan in motion.

I got dressed in my sexiest pajamas and looked outside. Jake wasn't home.

"You need to move your car," I told him.

"True. Aight, hit my phone. Act like you gotta hit the bathroom and text me." He left, and I stared out the window until I saw Jake's car pull in.

I didn't even understand why he needed dope when my father was Marsel Standfield. He was just greedy.

I walked out to act like I was grabbing the mail and then put on a show like I locked my door with the key in it.

"You good?" Jake came across the street.

"Yeah. I locked my key in the house. I was about to get the mail." I looked at the house.

"Ain't none of them unlocked?" he asked, looking at my thighs.

"Nope."

"Well, sit over there with me, and I can get you a locksmith," he offered.

"I got my phone. I can do it." I showed him.

"Well, come over anyway." He smirked.

"You know we ain't getting' down like that." I squinted at him.

"Shid, you know this dick was in them guts. You fuckin' with that lame ass nigga again, though, right?" he said, and I rolled my eyes.

"I need to use the bathroom anyway," I said.

"Come on, then." Jake rubbed his hands together, and we walked across the street. He let us into his house.

I knew where his bathroom was, so I went and texted Tonka. I flushed the toilet like I had used it and walked out.

When I got to the living room, Jake was smoking. I sat next to him and snatched the blunt out of his hand.

"Really, ma?" he said, now looking at my titties.

"Nigga, stop bein' a creep," I told him.

"You know you came out when you saw me." He rubbed up and down my thigh.

"You wish, Jake." I laughed, and he went higher.

"You already wet." He made it to my pussy, and he had me creamy than a bitch.

"I'm always wet." I blew the smoke, and he pushed his fingers into my pussy.

"Damn." He kissed between my cleavage.

"Bend over," he demanded.

I kept the blunt and did what he said, because, in a minute, Tonka was gon' walk in on me fucking the shit out of him. That ten inches was calling me now that I had seen it.

I heard him unwrap a condom and in went the dick. I started to throw it back and puff the blunt, holding it in while he dug into me deeply.

"Fuck," I choked.

He grabbed my ass and began to pound harder and harder.

We were definitely enjoying each other when the door flew open, and two masked gunmen came in. I knew one of them was Tonka.

"Get the fuck down!" Tonka screamed, and I recognized his voice.

"Man, shit." Jake looked at me, and I was crying like I was terrified.

"It's aight, do what they say," he said to me.

I saw that my little show had convinced him that I wasn't involved.

"Take me to the safe, nigga," Tonka said.

Jake did what they said, and they walked out with big ass duffle bags.

After they left, I stayed tied up downstairs with Jake, and he asked me over and over if I had something to do with it. I had to convince him that I was a victim like he was. He said he had a son and a wife in Jamaica who were coming here to live next month, so now he needed to move, so they wouldn't be in danger. He was a trifling ass nigga, out here fucking on me and whoever else with a whole family.

A few days later, I was pissed off, walking back and forth through my house and wondering where the fuck this nigga Tonka was. He disappeared and got low on my ass. I was so mad that I did what I needed to in order to get his attention. He wasn't gonna use me to come up and then cut me out.

I went to Jake and told him that I found out Tonka robbed him and gave the money and shit to Queen. He trusted me, even more, when he saw me tell him the truth about a nigga who I so called loved. I didn't even know he and Queen were broken up at the time. That's why Tonka was so back in love with me, and I realized that.

I decided to follow Jake when he told me he was going over there, and when I saw him shoot the house up, I sped off. After I saw what happened to Queen and her son, I felt this guilt because I put the wheels in motion. I honestly just thought if Tonka knew Jake was looking for him, he would come to me.

The very next day, I got a call from Tonka saying to meet him at the airport. He told me to pack and grab a passport. When I got to Miami International, he was there waiting for me.

"We gotta get the fuck. Base told me that nigga came to the trap and shit looking for me. How the fuck this nigga know we did that shit?" he asked me.

"How the fuck am I supposed to know, nigga? I'm scared for my life now too." I played my part.

"Look, we going to the Dominican Republic for a minute. I had money wired to an account. My aunt helped me."

"What about Queen?" I asked.

"She said we done, so we done. Fuck her. All I'm worried about is my son," he said.

I didn't tell him what I knew just yet.

Tonka told me we would change our identities while we were there. He thought we could get money moving weight out there and bring the money back into the US when shit got cool again. My new name was Sonovia, but he kept my last name the same. It wasn't until a few months after we left the country that he found out his son was gone. He was upset like Queen should have informed him, and even I had to remind him that we were off the fucking grid. The only reason he found out is that he finally got a phone and called his ugly ass grandmother.

We stayed in the Dominican Republic for three years. I couldn't lie and say they were perfect, but it was close. Tonka had this change in him, and it was nice. He needed to get away from Miami, and he was amazing without them streets. We even got married and planned to have kids. Everything was good until he got a call from one of his loser ass folks, telling him that Jake been dead, and he could come back. I begged him to stay in the DR, and he insisted on going back. He said he just wanted to visit, and we would come home. I made it back, but he never made it back with me.

One night, he got drunk at his aunt's house, and his cousins were talking about his old partner, Base, and how he was with Queen now. Why the fuck was everything about this bitch?

They told him how he had money and the streets on lock, and that's when everything changed in Tonka's mind.

"Let's go get some of that money then!" he said, but I knew this was about Queen.

"You just want payback for that bitch," I said as he got his cousins all hype and shit.

"Drive." He threw me the keys to his Impala.

I took a deep breath and had a bad ass feeling about this bullshit. When we got on this dark ass block, his cousin pulled their Lincoln over.

His cousin Blue got out and came to my window.

"Aight, we gon' go first. I see some nigga out there and a bitch. We can shoot they ass down and ransack it," he said.

"That's a bet." Tonka nodded.

As we approached, I realized it was Queen.

"Look at this bitch," Tonka said as he watched Base and Queen kissing, and Base watched Queen's ass while she walked.

The shots began, and I hit the corner hard, almost running into a parked car. Tonka got out and started shooting, and I sat shaking in the car.

I saw Queen shooting, and I slid down in my seat.

I honked the horn for Tonka to run and get in, but she shot him down. I saw her ready to shoot at the car, so I pulled off. Before I hit the right, I saw her stomping him in the face. I knew he was gonna die, and I screamed as I drove to the nearest alley and cried my eyes out.

Things were going so well, and I wished we could have stayed away. I heard Base got killed too, so that was some consolation, but it wasn't even. She took him from me two times, and I couldn't let her ass just be. I went back to The

DR and fell into the deepest depression. I got surgery on my face just to make a change, and I liked it. I got my titties done, too, and I legally changed my name to Sonovia as a reminder of me and Tonka's time.

After a year, I went home and introduced my new self to my family. When I heard my father was doing business with Queen, my blood boiled. I put my whole plan in motion after she got into it with my brothers. Can you imagine them calling this bitch The Queen? Fuck her, I was The Queen, and after I took that bitch down, I would show everybody that hell hath no fury like a woman scorned.

Queen

"Hey, Ma," I said as I walked into my mother's one-story house in Little Havana.

I had made sure she was set up since she'd been out. She ran the beauty shop in jail, so I got her a shop of her own once she got out. I let her pick the location and everything. It was upscale, and she ran a whole make up bar. My mother did a damn good job too. She never mentioned the ugliness of our past, and I was grateful. I felt guilty enough, and I was trying to make it up to her every day.

"You look good." She hugged me and handed me a wine glass.

"Where's Terrance?" I looked around and saw that her new husband wasn't home.

She had gotten married last year, and they were cute. I could tell he loved my mother.

"He went to play grab ass with his friends," she said as she poured me some wine.

"Um, what?" I laughed.

"He went to the university homecoming. You know Miami U is his alma matter," she said.

"Don't be like that. He's just there to support his school," I told her and sipped from my glass.

"Girl, bye, I ain't no fool. They out there looking at that scattered ass." She looked out front and saw my white Rolls Royce then shook her head.

"I can't believe my baby is so powerful." She looked at Vixie, one of my main guards, who stood next to me most of the time. She was in the doorway, leaning against the wall.

"You got a driver and security," she said as she sat next to me, "but no man. Shit, or woman. I know you go both ways," she said.

"Ma, don't go there with the gay speeches. You knew this," I said.

"I ain't say shit was wrong. I licked some pussy in jail. It's okay," she said.

I prayed God would scrub it from my memory and the visual that came with it.

"That's good to know, Ma, but I got people I deal with. I'm fine. I don't have to have somebody."

"I know, but it would be nice to have a grandchild... another one," she said.

I licked my lip and gulped down the rest of the wine, finishing the glass.

"I will in time," I told her.

"You ready for lunch?" I asked.

"Yeah, let me get my shoes." She got up and ran up the stairs.

I opened my phone and saw a message from Tevony that she needed to talk to me. I didn't want to handle business when I was trying to spend time with my mother, but if it was about whoever touched Wessie, I needed to know.

"Aye, Ma, I need to make a stop real fast," I told her.

"Okay, but don't be taking me to no drug deal," she said.

"I'm past all that, Ma." I laughed.

She still somehow thought I met in shady buildings and exchanged money. I was business partners with Marsel now. He was no longer my connect; I was the connect. He played the background, but with him getting older, he often talked about retiring. I didn't wanna have to work with his sons because I would have to kill their asses. We had grown to have that father-daughter relationship, the father I always wanted.

"I'm ready." My mother walked out with me.

Vexie opened the door for us and then got in the passenger side.

My mother put her seat belt on and tapped Emily, my driver.

"Don't be driving like no fool while I'm in this bitch," she complained before Emily even put the car in drive.

"Ma, sit back. Emily, we're going to Tevony's," I told her.

We drove, and my mother talked about her and Terrance's trip to Paris in a few months. I was glad she finally got the man she deserved. Educated, kind, and not a drug addict.

"Wait here, mother." I got out, and Vixie came out behind me.

We walked up to the building. Vixie opened the door, and I walked past the lobby.

"Ms. Malone. How are you?" Sephia, the concierge, spoke.

I waved and walked to the elevator. I owned this building, and I often helped my employees be more accessible by housing them. Of course, they paid rent and all, but I paid them enough to live comfortably like this with crazy money to spare.

I got off the elevator and rang the doorbell. Tevony opened the door, and Vixie walked in before me then looked behind the door.

"Hey, Queen. I know you were spending time with your mother, but you might wanna hear this shit."

She picked up a folder and handed it to me.

"I got the file from Wessie's shooting. Since he refused to cooperate, they had to pull surveillance. The police file says it was a black Impala that drove around the block two times before the shooting took place. They're looking for the driver but get this shit. The car was registered to a dead man." She handed me the DMV record.

I felt like my world began to spin when I saw the name on the papers.

"Ja'Sean Pike," I said aloud, and my heart rate began to speed up.

"You okay, Queen?" Tevony asked me.

"Yeah. Thanks." I took the papers with me out the door. Anything she had to say after that would fall on deaf ears.

Ja'Sean Pike was Tonka's government name. Who the fuck would be driving a car in his name?

The rest of the day was nothing but deep thoughts.

When I met up with Parquita to talk about how we would be changing the distro schedule, I wasn't all there.

"You good over there?" she asked as I looked at how much dope we had about to come through.

"Yeah, I'm okay. Check this shit out, though." I turned to her. "The police got an Impala registered to Tonka that was at the scene when Wessie got shot."

"Huh? But didn't you—"

"Yeah, I did, so that shit got my head fucked up right now. I got one of those feelings," I told her.

"Aye, shit, last time you had one of those feelings, we ended up having to take a whole crew down," Parquita said.

"I know, but I feel it. Some shit about to go down," I told her.

Parquita came up and turned me to her.

"Queen, it ain't shit they can do in these streets that's gon make you, us, and anybody associated with you fold. You know I got you," she said, and I nodded.

"Thanks, boo," I said as she took her seat.

"So, how that shit with you and Ms. Boogie comin'?" I asked, talking about her fiancée Brandy.

"Shit, we good. Shawty tryna take all my money with this wedding though," she said, and I laughed.

"Man, that's what women do. We spend money. Shit, you a stud, but even you blow bags," I said, and she laughed.

"Yeah, well, I'll give her whatever she wants, so she good," she said.

I envied that. I wish I wasn't cursed because I wanted to be in love again.

"Must be nice," I told her.

"You can have that shit, too, Queen."

"Nah, you know that love shit never works out for me. Let's finish this shit up."

I went back to arranging drops with her since she was also my head of distribution. My mind was going a hundred different places, but what kept coming back was Tonka's car and the fact that it looked just like the car I saw that night I killed him. Yeah, some shit was going down, but like Parquita said, I don't fold.

***

I sat in the ballroom, looking around at all of Marsel's constituents talking and pretending like they weren't the most illegal niggas in Florida. Marsel had a ball every single year to celebrate his and my success, but this time, I wasn't as interested. After wondering if I actually killed Tonka entered my mind, I couldn't let it rest. I just knew he was dead at the time, but now I didn't know shit. For the moment, I had to leave it and come back.

"Queen, you okay? You're quiet tonight." Marsel's wife, Christi, touched my hand.

She was my age, and she and Marsel had been married for two years. His first wife, his scum ass kids' mother, died of breast cancer a few years back.

"I'm fine. Just a little tired," I told her.

"Well, after this morning." Presia, my date, rubbed my leg under the table.

I had been dealing with Presia for a year, and she was beautiful inside and out. She had worked for me for a while, and now I let her run one of my daycares. She was in love with me, and I had love for her too.

"You two are so cute together," Kristi said, beaming at Presia and me.

"Thanks." I smiled and saw Wessie walk in the room with Sonovia.

This was the first time she had ever come to one of these, but I knew why she did. Just to show off Wessie to me, she came walking through like Ms. America and shit. They approached the table, and I took Presia by the hand and led her to the dance floor.

"So, you're not tired anymore?" Presia kissed my neck.

I ran my hands down her ass and rubbed as we danced.

"I wasn't tired, just got a lot of shit on my mind. That's a typical response when I don't feel like talking," I told her.

"Damn, you need to put some dick in your life, shawty." Malcom walked by and grabbed his dick, looking at Presia.

"You and your four-inch dick could never," I spat and mugged him.

"Enjoy all that slick shit, Queen. My father about to announce some shit that's gon' shut you the fuck up," he said, and I looked at him with a smirk.

Poor little suburban boy who liked to play with the streets.

"I can't stand them," Presia said in my ear.

"Don't worry 'bout them. He's the one in for a surprise." I smirked as Marsel waved me up.

I kissed Presia, and she went back to her seat. As I walked up, I saw Wessie looking at me from his seat with Sonovia.

"Okay, let me go ahead and get it started. I wanted to announce this later in the night, but I wanna do it now, so we can get it out the way." Marsel grabbed my hand as I walked up the stairs.

His sons stood next to him, and they looked like it was Christmas morning.

"As a lot of you know, I've been in this game for a long time. I'm finally finished," Marsel said, and people began to gasp.

"Man, Marsel, we don't trust nobody but you and Queen," Charles, one of our customers, called out.

"You gonna let me finish?" Marsel asked him.

"Go 'head, Pops," Malcom said with a big smile.

"As I was saying, I'm finished. Queen is now your connect. I handed everything over to her, and since you trust her, the transition should be nice and smooth," Marsel said.

"What the fuck!" Toreese spat.

"You gave our family business to this bitch?" Malcom asked him, and everybody looked around.

My girls had already started to make their way to the front.

I put my hand up to stop them.

"You know I'm tired of that mouth of yours." I looked at both Malcom and Toreese.

"This ain't the place," Marsel interjected.

"So, where's the place, so I can be there?" Malcom asked.

"I said what I had to say. You want work, it's through Queen or find another plug," Marsel told them.

"Man, fuck this shit. We your fucking blood." Toreese angrily stepped to Marsel, who didn't take that kindly.

I watched him knock the shit out of Toreese in front of the whole room.

"You wanna do it here? Cool. I ain't handing my legacy over to some niggas who don't know shit about what it means to sit on the top. Y'all never wanted to learn shit. You only wanted fast money. You'd be dead or in jail within a year if I would have put the crown on your head. This *bitch,* as y'all like to call her, can teach you some shit about what it means to be a real fucking boss. She never got locked up, and she moved more weight than either of you could imagine in your wet ass dreams. Put some fucking respect on her name, and if I hear anything about you not respecting her past this day, you finna deal with me. Period," Marsel said, and I felt myself getting emotional.

"QUEEN!" somebody yelled out, and then it erupted through the room. Everybody held their glass up, and so did I.

"I love you like a daughter. You're a great leader already, Queen." Marsel hugged me, and I saw Sonovia turn red as I hugged him back.

Malcom and Toreese stormed out, and the night continued.

"I hope I didn't cause any problems with your family," I told Marsel as we walked out the door arm in arm. We often walked that way as we talked.

"No, it was bound to happen, I would have rather stayed in the game than to hand anything over to them. They aren't ready for this," he said.

"I won't let you down," I told him as we made it outside the hotel where our cars waited in front.

I noticed that I had left my damn phone, so I went to see if the people cleaning up had grabbed it.

"Get in the car with Vixie," I told Presia.

When I walked back into the ballroom, I could hear arguing in the back of the room.

"Fuck you. I'm going home with my father," I heard Sonovia say as she walked out the side door without even noticing me.

I tried to remain still so he wouldn't see me either, but he did.

"So, you just enjoying the show?" Wessie asked me.

"I came in here because I left my phone," I told him. I was happy to see it was still on my chair.

"I guess I ain't get to congratulate," Wessie said as I tried to move through the tables. He came and stopped my path.

"You got everything you wanted. You stayed in the game, and now you on the very top," Wessie said, and I could hear the sarcasm dripping from his voice.

"But what?"

"No buts, I'm happy for you, and I see you still got good taste in women," he said, obviously talking about Presia.

"Of course. I see you still have shitty taste in women."

"Does that include you?" He smirked.

"Whatever, Wessie. You just Mr. Perfect, huh?" I wasn't about to stand there and do this with his ass. "Look, I gotta go." I tried to pass him, but he stopped me.

"How long you been havin' folks following me?" he asked.

"As long as I wanted them to, but don't worry. You got a wife to look after you now, so they won't bother you anymore," I lied.

I would always make sure he was okay no matter how fucked up he was with me.

"Queen, you coming?" Presia walked in and smiled at Wessie.

"Hi," she spoke, and he looked her up and down.

"Wassup, sweetheart? I'm Wessie." He shook her hand.

"Damn, this brings back some memories." Wessie bit his lip and walked past me, rubbing his hand across my leg by accident, but it still felt good to even feel his body.

When I turned around, he was looking at us as he left out. I always kept a bitch, even when I was dealing with a nigga sexually. So, of course, Wessie got to enjoy two women at once sometimes when we would fuck. To be honest, that shit played a part in our destruction; he stopped wanting to share me.

"He fine as hell, Queen," Presia said, and I nodded.

"That, he is." I walked out hand in hand with her.

I spotted Wessie walking to the driver's side of a Porsche. Looking at him, I felt that it was time to reveal things that, even during our short relationship, he never knew. He had to understand me.

"Hold on." I walked away from the car.

"Wessie," I called out right before he closed his door.

He got out and waited for me to speak my piece.

"I didn't have an abortion to hurt you. My son was murdered in front of me. Ever since then, I've felt this guilt about replacing him, and I made a fucked-up choice. I lost my brother and three of the loves of my life. My son, Base, he loved me like you love me, the last one is you, Wessie. I have to deal with all of that every day, knowing the last one was my fault. I didn't have control over the other shit, but you, I fucked you up for me. I just wanted to say that to get it off my chest and let you know you can hate me, but just know I left because I loved you, boy. I loved you like a mufucka."

I couldn't believe I had tears running down my face as I stood in the street, spilling my heart, knowing it couldn't mean shit but an apology.

Wessie stood there, looking dumbfounded.

I felt embarrassed, so I walked away.

"I could never hate you," he said, and I stopped and looked at him.

"So, can we just be cool now?" I walked back over to where he was standing.

"I could never just be cool with you either." He grabbed my neck and parted my lips with his tongue, then took my breath away.

"Wessie, stop." I stepped back, but he pulled me right back to him, and we kept kissing.

"Why wasn't I invited?" Presia said as she walked up.

"Nah, that was a goodbye, and I forgive you, kiss," Wessie said to her.

"Too bad." She gave him the fuck me eyes.

"Go," I told her.

She pouted and walked away.

"So, you forgive me? That's what that was?" I asked him.

"Yeah, that and some other shit I needed to get off my chest with you. I appreciate your honesty, though, ma." He stroked my face and got in his car.

My legs were so weak, I couldn't even move, but I pretended to stand there for dramatics because a bitch was stuck. He was the only nigga besides Base who could have me like this. I guess I felt better knowing he forgave me, but damn, that kiss, though.

***

"Nah, Trisha, you done." I pointed out that she reneged.

"I saw that shit too," Parquita said.

We were playing spades and taking some time off to relax. I was tired from all the extra shit I had to do now that I was head of the organization. As the new head, I had to meet people I never heard of in countries I hadn't planned to visit. I even had to get a translator to travel with me. I didn't know the drug trade extended as far as it did, but I definitely saw some shit. Marsel was still mentoring me from afar through secure video chats. He had his own special shit built for us to do that.

"Come on, Queen, take the books," Brandy said.

"Don't worry, I'm collecting," I told her.

"That shit finna be ours." Parquita slapped hands with me.

"It's still gonna be mine, one way or another," Brandy said and kissed Parquita.

"See, that's why I ain't getting married." I laughed.

"Oh, we know, Queen. I'm gonna die waiting for a son-in-law and another grandchild that I can claim," my mother called from the kitchen.

"Thanks, Ma," I said.

"So, y'all gonna act like I'm not an option?" Presia said.

"No. My daughter is marrying a man," my mother came out of the kitchen and said.

"Damn, Queen, you just finna sit there?" Presia asked.

"You know we ain't even on that level. Don't act all funny cuz people here," I said to her, and she rolled her eyes.

"But she's always with you, so she might as well be your wife," Trisha said.

"Look, come on," I said, getting them to focus back on the game.

We ran a few more hands, and Parquita and I cleaned all them bundles off the table. They only won one game.

"Queen, we got two hours until we have to meet up with that new guy Marsel just took on before he left." Tevony walked in with her glasses at the tip of her nose.

"Aight."

We went out back before I got ready to fall out. Tisha and my mother had left, and Brandy took Presia home for me while Parquita and I rode out. I had to go change first, so I could get into my Queenliness.

I went up the stairs and laid out the white and gold catsuit with one of my favorite white mink stoles.

After I was done, I went downstairs.

Parquita fake bowed, and I smacked my teeth.

"Girl." I laughed, and she got up, then we walked out to get in the car.

"Did you take care of that chick who was in front of the pizza spot?" I asked Parquita.

We were walking into one of the pizza shops I owned downtown, and a woman was sitting outside with two kids. She said she didn't have a place, and they were hungry. That shit moved me, and I asked Parquita to make sure she got in one of the women shelters that I had opened on this side.

"Yeah, but she was full of shit," she said as the car pulled off.

"What you mean?" I asked.

"That bitch wasn't homeless. She stays in that new high rise in the west. She's a professional scammer."

"Man, and she got them kids out there doin' that bullshit. I been hoping they was aight all this time. I hate bitches who use their kids as pawns and shit," I said, angry at the shit now.

"Me too, that's why I pulled up on her ass and told her I would call CPS if I saw her out there again," Parquita said.

"Good. Weak ass bitch."

I looked out the window and thought about kids who had to go through worse. I honestly felt like if I didn't make that move on my pops, we would have been in a worse situation, and since my mother refused to leave, she would have let it happen.

I saw my phone ringing and wondered who the hell could be calling my phone. I didn't know, but I felt like I needed to answer.

"Who is this?" I picked up and asked.

"Queen, I need your help." I heard Presia crying on the phone.

"What's wrong?" I was alert.

"They say they gonna kill me if you don't come."

"Who? You home, baby?"

"Tell her to stop asking so many questions," I heard an unfamiliar deep voice say.

I tapped Tevony and grabbed her phone then wrote in text for her to send some bitches to Presia's house.

"What they want?" I asked.

"They just want you to come." She cried harder.

"We want you to take her place. Her life for yours." The nigga must have taken the phone.

"When will y'all ever learn?" I said as Tevony put the thumbs up to tell me that our girls were there already. I had goons everywhere, so it was nothing to have somebody touched in less than five minutes.

"Cool, let's just kill this bitch," she said.

As Presia screamed her lungs out, I heard gunshots. The fact that she was still screaming let me know my people were already there, and she was okay.

"Presia," I called out, and I heard shuffling.

"Queen." She picked up.

"Oh my God, they tried to kill me," she said.

"You aight?" I asked.

"Yeah, I just... what the fuck?" she cried.

"Just go with my people, and you'll be aight," I told her.

"Okay."

She hung up, and I wondered who the fuck would try this. I automatically thought about Malcom and Toreese trying to get payback for losing the empire to me. I mean, if it was, Marsel would be burying their ass.

Everything goes out the window when you tell me you want my life. I had put a security detail on Presia to make sure nothing like this happened again. I made sure she didn't see them, so she could act normally, and if somebody did come, they would think shit was sweet.

When they showed me the dudes' faces, I didn't recognize them, but I would find out who the fuck they were soon enough.

Queen

"You sure about this shit?" I asked Parquita as I looked at the reports from the last collection.

"I'm positive, Queen. It's over two hundred stacks missing." She shook her head.

"You know this shit never gets old. Every year, somebody thinks they're smarter than me because I have titties. I just..."

I laughed, looking at how Brady did it. This nigga stole five thousand dollars from multiple accounts and didn't think we would see it because of the millions blinding us. I didn't give a fuck if it was three dollars, it was fucking mine!

"OFF WITH HIS HEAD." I got up from the Golden throne and walked down the stairs.

Call me dramatic, but I had a golden throne shipped from Egypt, and I enjoyed sitting on it while making decisions like this. It made me feel like the queen I was.

When we got into my Purple Bentley, I decided to ride in the passenger seat instead of the back.

"Queen, I got Vixie on the phone. She said he just walked in with a female," Parquita told me.

"Oh, goody, collateral damage." I rolled my eyes.

Brady worked as an accountant. When we got our dope money from the dealers, we gave it to him to clean, and he put it in my corporate business account. I owned a radio station and a television production company, and the money flowed through them. I knew he would eventually get greedy, just not this soon.

"Nice." I looked at the building that I had only seen from a distance in pictures. I knew where everybody who worked for me lived; even if I had never been there, I knew what it looked like.

I walked in and smiled at the little girl playing with her dog in the lobby.

"You're beautiful," I told her, then pulled out a one-hundred-dollar bill from my purse and gave it to her.

"This is all that matters. Make more of it when you grow up." I smiled and got on the elevator.

When we got to the penthouse, I looked at the door and then at Parquita.

She stood back and kicked the door in. That bitch was strong.

When we walked in, all I could hear were moans of pleasure coming from the back.

"Oh, he's getting some pussy," I said, admiring how nice his place was for a man.

When I got to the bedroom, I saw legs in the air, and Brady was fucking her good; I could tell.

"Ahhhhh!" she screamed when she saw me standing there.

Brady turned around and covered them up.

"Oh no, don't worry, we'll wait." I put my hands up and looked at my girls.

"Queen, I..." Brady started, but I tapped Parquita, who raised her gun.

"I said we'll wait. Keep going." I sat in the armchair in the corner, and he looked confused.

"What's going on?" The white chick looked scared as hell.

"Dick in pussy. That's what's going on. I don't want to interrupt. So, Brady, please continue or get a bullet."

They were shaking as he climbed back on her.

I wanted to laugh, but I had to keep a straight face for effect. He was fucking her and looked at me as if to say, 'Am I doing good?'

"Woooooh, get her, daddy!" I said as he pounded harder and harder.

After about five minutes, I assumed he had cum, and he got up.

"Okay, so now can you tell me what the hell is going on?" he asked.

"Yeah, this." I popped him two times in the head with my .22.

"Oh, no, please." The chick stood up, and I almost shot her until I saw her body.

"Damn." I got up and looked at her. "You pretty as fuck." I went and stroked her face.

"Thank you." She was shivering.

"See, I could kill you, right? In fact, I should kill you right now."

"God, no, I'm scared." She backed up.

"When the last time you been to the clinic?" I asked her.

"Huh?"

"The clinic!" I barked, and she jumped.

"Last week, I had a pap smear." She folded her arms.

"Okay, you're going again. Parquita, take this bitch to the clinic, get her cleaned up, and drop her off at my house tonight." I walked out and went back downstairs to get in the car.

Parquita walked to the Navigator behind me and put the chick in it.

I saw my phone ringing, and it felt weird to see the number because I knew exactly who it was.

"Wessie?" I picked up.

"Damn, I didn't know you had my number," he said.

"Yeah, well, you know."

"I need to see you."

"You need to see me?" I asked, wondering why.

The last time I saw him, he said it was goodbye, and now he needs to see me?

"Okay," I simply stated.

"I'm at your house," he said and hung up.

When I got to my home, I only had Vixie with me. She got out and looked at the BMW sitting in my driveway.

I walked up and saw the window rolled down.

Vixie pulled me back in case somebody was about to shoot.

"It's me," Wessie said, and Vixie relaxed.

When he got out, I saw Priest and Vibe step out with him.

"Hey?" I asked more like a question.

"Wassup, Queen?" Priest nodded.

Wessie just sat there like he really didn't wanna be there, which hurt a little. I thought he was calling for a different reason. He got out, and we all walked into my house.

"Shit, Queen," Vibe said as he looked around.

"Like y'all not living lovely out in Cali," I said, knowing these niggas lived like kings.

As we entered my living room, Vibe walked in behind me and began to talk.

"We got an issue," Vibe said, and I wondered what their issues had to do with me.

"You still got connections to my family back in Greece?" Wessie asked, and my stomach tightened.

"Not anymore. Why?"

"We got shot at back home. We got them, but we saw the Greek flag tattooed on one of them," Priest said.

"You flew from Oakland to ask about the Greeks?" I asked Priest and Vibe.

"You know I don't play about my sisters, Queen. I cut ties with them, so I have no inside knowledge of why they would be doing this, especially knowing who my father and grandfather were," Wessie said.

I really couldn't believe how oblivious he was to his own situation. That's why I would never turn my back on him; he needed me.

"I can find something out for you. I got you," I told Wessie.

"It's not about me, it's about my sisters." He got up.

"Hold up. Priest and Vibe, I'll send some people to Oakland. You don't have to worry about the shit ever again. I know y'all can handle your own, but these Greeks are on a different type of bullshit."

"We appreciate it, Queen." Priest kissed my hand, and I smiled.

"Aight, I'ma see y'all later." Wessie got up, and I just wasn't having it.

"Wow, only calling when you need something. Typical nigga." I angrily stood and walked past him to let them out.

Wessie grabbed my arms, and I saw Poet and Neak, my guards who stood at the door, approach. I held my hand up.

"Y'all know you don't touch him," I said to them, and they backed off.

Vibe and Priest stepped outside to give us a minute.

I pulled Wessie into the corner, and he just looked down at me.

"Can you honestly say you hate me?" I touched his chest, and he looked away.

"I told you I don't." He looked back at me, and I just wanted to suck on his bottom lip.

"Then why you still being so cold, Wessie?" I accidentally bumped his stomach, and he winced in pain.

I lifted his shirt and saw that his wounds were still bandaged.

"How you feel?" I pulled him back onto the couch and lifted the bandages.

"Wessie, this shit looks infected," I said.

"I'm aight, Queen," he said like he was aggravated.

"No, you're not." I picked up my phone and called my personal doctor.

"I need to go," he said, and I grabbed his keys.

"No." I tossed them to Neak, and she walked out the door with them.

"Queen, I ain't for no bullshit right now," he said.

"Me either, that's why the fuck you gonna stay until my doctor comes and checks you out. I don't care how much you don't wanna be around me, I ain't letting shit happen to you, Wessie," I said.

I wished he knew how much I loved him, so he could stop being so mad.

"It's funny, Queen, like I keep saying. Where was all this care before?"

"And like I keep saying, it never left," I told him.

He leaned his head back, and I could tell he was still in a lot of pain and probably shouldn't be out and about. He moved me and tried to get up.

"Why don't you call your wife and tell her to come and take you to a fucking hospital since you don't wanna be here with me trying to help."

"Because she only makes shit worse," he said.

I could tell he didn't mean to say that, at least not to me.

"Well, that's who you chose," I said, and he looked at me with a scowl.

"Nah, it wasn't." He looked out the window, and his car was gone, so were Priest and Vibe. "Where that bitch take my car?"

"I didn't take your car anywhere, and I would appreciate not being called a bitch. Your brothers in law took it after I told them we would take you home," Neak said.

"Man, fuck, you still gotta rule everybody and everything, huh?" He looked at me.

"Well, since you see it ain't gonna change, sit down." I put a slight smile on, and he lay back on my chaise.

After about twenty minutes of silence, Wessie had gotten bored and started to watch TV. Flipping through channels, he landed on The Wayans brothers because, for some reason, they played that shit all day on TV, that and Martin.

"Damn, Pops was old as fuck forever," he said, and I took that as an opening for a conversation.

"I know. I mean, I've never seen him young." I laughed, and so did he.

"Him or Samuel L Jackson," he agreed, and I accidentally touched his hands while laughing.

He looked down at my hand over his, and somehow, our fingers locked. We sat holding hands for like thirty seconds until Vixie announced that Dr. Bright was there, and we quickly let each other go.

I knew I was right about Wessie's condition. He was infected and needed antibiotics immediately.

"You're lucky she called me. I've seen things like this turn deadly." Dr. Bright handed Wessie a bottle of pills and gave me a bill for his door service. His old, dusty ass was expensive, but he was worth every penny of his fee. He carried his own pharmacy in his van and all.

"I got it." Wessie went into his pocket and tossed him a bankroll. "Can I leave now, or you still tryna hold a nigga hostage?" he asked.

"Drop him off," I told Emily, who was sitting in the hallway.

"Aye, Queen."

I turned to Wessie after he called out to me.

"I do feel better, though, thank you." He winked and left out the door.

I was starting to believe there was nothing I could do to get him not to have that grudge against me, but I could tell his wall was starting to come back down

Wessie

"Aw, shit." I grabbed the end of the bed and pounded deep into Sonovia as she threw her ass back at me.

I watched her bounce on my dick, and that shit almost had me ready to cum, but I was drunk as fuck and ready to go all night. The fact that she was nice and wet for a nigga had me on go too.

"Yes, daddy, buss it open. Shit!" she screamed, talking nasty to me like I liked.

I gripped her ass and forced her on her stomach. Her ass looked so good that I wanted to fuck it. I pulled out of her pussy and started to push into her ass. She held her cheeks open for me. I slid into her ass, and I lay on her, hitting her with close strokes so deep she was gasping.

I pulled out and lay down, pulling her on top. I wanted her to ride it with the dick in her ass. I turned her in reverse cowgirl and watched my dick go back in. I laid back and watched her do her thing until I was ready to cum.

Ding Dong

"Who the fuck is that?" Sonovia got up, and I looked out the window.

"Aw, shit, that's Jacca. Why the fuck the nigga ain't call first?" I grabbed my phone and went to the security app.

"Aye, holdup, cuz," I said through the speaker.

I washed my dick off and grabbed my sweats. When I came out, Sonovia wasn't in the room any longer.

When I got downstairs, she was in my tank top with no pants on or bra.

"Go put some fuckin' clothes on," I spat as Jacca watched her go up the stairs.

"You here for a reason besides being up shawty's ass?" I used my thumb to point up the stairs where Sonovia went.

"I couldn't say it on the phone. I saw some of Queen's people on the block. I can't say if they were selling, but they were posted. I know you still got that agreement and shit, so I was wondering if you wanted us to approach them or just chill on the shit." He clasped his hands.

"Nah, don't approach. Either they ain't with her no more, or they stupid. But, my nigga, you could have waited to tell me that shit," I said.

"Nah, nigga, you told me when I got here that anything out of place is a problem. It looked like they were scoping the block and how we moved.

"Tell you what, ride down on the rest of the blocks in Little Havana that you cover, and if you see anybody else, let me know because that would be too much of a coincidence," I told him.

"I figured you would say that, and I did. It was two more sitting on each block," he said.

"Oh, okay, well damn. I guess I gotta go speak to the Queen."

"Well, if you do, I'm going too." Sonovia rushed down and said.

"This ain't got shit to do with you, and stop eavesdropping on business," I told her.

"You think you so fucking slick. You just tryna be around her, Wessie," Sonovia said, and my dick was no longer any use to her tonight. When she got into that attitude, I couldn't fuck her because it turned me the fuck off.

"You ain't hearing what the fuck going on, or you just heard Queen, and ran your mufuckin' ass down here?"

"That was it," Jacca said and laughed.

"Shut your black ass up," she spat at him and mugged us as she went back up the stairs.

"I'll holla at her. Don't shoot unless them niggas do."

I slapped hands with him and went upstairs to go the fuck to sleep and hit Queen to see what the fuck was going on. She agreed to see me and told me one of her girls would pick me up tomorrow.

***

"Baby girl, you gon' be beating my dick in a minute if you slide over my shit one more time," I told one of Queen's guards, who was only searching me for pleasure at this point.

"He clean." She looked at me and pursed her lips.

"You knew that four minutes of the five you were rubbing me down," I said to her and walked through the big ass mansion that was just as nice as the one she had on the beach. Damn, shawty had crazy taste in real estate.

"The indoor pool is that way." The chick pointed, and I could see the water reflecting off the walls through the ceiling high double doors.

When I walked in, I saw Queen floating on a large floatation lounge with angel wings on the back. She always swam nude, so I wasn't surprised to see her perfect body exposed.

I couldn't stop thinking about what she had told me; I couldn't imagine losing a kid like that. I even looked into the shit, and it was way more fucked up when you knew the details. She had definitely been through some shit, but she didn't look like it at all.

"So, you really that scared of me that you finna stay in the pool?" I asked.

"Wessie, I have never been scared of shit. I was already chillin'," she said.

I walked to where she was floating and saw that there was a line attached to her float. I reeled her in, and she took a deep breath then slid off, getting into the water. She walked out, looking like a commercial.

"Okay, that's better." I watched her pick up a towel and dry her legs off.

"Wessie, wassup?" She sat down, and I sat next to her.

"You put some niggas on our blocks to watch us?" I asked her straight up.

"That's really a question for me?" She looked offended that I would think she would try to cut in on me.

"Yesterday, we had a few dudes who were recognized as your boys," I said.

"I doubt it. You forgot I don't run corner boys or girls no more. I'm strictly weight," she told me.

"So, we clear to drop any niggas who used to work for you? Because they out there watching the shit, and now I feel they on bullshit," I told her.

"Do what you gotta do, nigga." She shrugged.

"Queen, they just brought your lunch. The caterer wants to set up in the main dining room," this lil' cute, geeky chick walked in and said.

"They can set it up in here," Queen told her.

"K." The girl nodded.

"Tevony, tell them to make sure they got utensils for two," Queen said.

"Is that a lunch invite?" I asked.

"No, I just like having extra silverware," she said in a slick ass tone.

"Yes or no?" I said, and she looked me up and down.

"I guess." She walked past me, and I grabbed her arm. Queen looked down, and I lifted her chin, but she looked away.

"Why the hell you grabbin' on me?" She finally looked at me.

"I'm sorry about all that shit that happened to you," I told her, and she pulled her lip in.

"Thanks, but I'm a lot better now. I just wish we'd had that conversation sooner." She licked her lips, and I had to fight myself.

I wanted her so bad, but I had to control myself. I stood there, rubbing her body up and down, and she felt perfect.

"You doin' it again." She broke our stare and embrace.

Queen picked her the remote and turned on the radio that played through the whole room. She grabbed a robe and closed it, covering nothing because the robe was sheer.

"What am I doin'?" I asked.

"Cheating on your wife, with your eyes and hands."

"Do it count if I can't stand her ass now?" I asked, and she laughed.

"Yeah, it counts." She shook her head.

The people were setting up the table for the food. My stomach was growling, and I didn't even know what the hell they had.

"You slobbing?" Queen sat at the table, and I joined her.

"Shit smells good," I said as they uncovered the food.

I was about to push them bitches out the way. Salmon, wild rice, crab cakes, and shrimp in some type of red buttery sauce.

"Man, I ain't eat shit yet." I grabbed a plate.

"They would have done it." Queen laughed and waved the women out.

"We can do it," I told her, and I made both our plates as Queen watched me.

"What?" I asked.

"I just think it's crazy that we're eating together. I thought this would just be some business transaction." She picked up her fork.

"Well, believe it, cuz I'm finna crush this shit, and you know I've never seen you as just business."

I started to eat, and we talked about shit like movies, avoiding actual real life shit. I could tell she wanted to say more, but I still enjoyed just having a regular conversation with no arguing and shit like it was with Sonovia.

"This was a hit!" I told her as I moved my second plate.

"I order from them all the time." Queen went to the small table next to her lounge chair and opened her cigarette case that was filled with joints.

"Let me know when, cuz, man." I held my stomach and realized I had been there for over an hour and a half.

"You ain't got no plans today?" Queen asked as she lay on the lounge, and I sat on the one next to her.

"You tryna kick me out?" I asked.

"No, nigga, I was just asking." She handed me the weed.

"Yeah, I got a few moves. I probably gotta go in a lil' bit." I looked at the time again.

"Yeah, me too. I got this meeting that I don't feel like going to," she said.

"You ain't got no nigga you get dick from?" I asked her, and she sat up and choked.

"Damn," I said as I tapped her back.

"Don't worry about it," she said, still choking.

"I mean, while you were watching me, I was watching you. You ain't had a nigga around," I told her, and she dropped her mouth.

"So, why were you watching me if you moved on?" she asked.

"Just like you, I wanted to make sure you were okay," I told her.

"And what did you find out?" She pulled another joint out; I could tell she was nervous.

"That you're lonely," I said, and her face looked devoid of feelings.

I had hit a nerve.

"I'm not fuckin' lonely, Wessie." She lit her weed and looked pissed now.

"You know I never gave a fuck about your attitude. I said what I said." I blew out the smoke.

"Well, so do you, nigga. Why the fuck you here with me when you got a wife? Why you put your lips on me, nigga? Because you lonely too, married and all." She got up, and I watched her grab the wine bottle out of the ice.

"Why you so mad?" I smirked.

It was something about getting one of the most powerful women I ever met in her feelings. For Queen, that wasn't easy. I had seen her take lives without a blink and stand up to niggas who could snap her in two.

She poured her glass, and before she could take a sip, I grabbed it from her hand.

"I ain't no fucked up dude, Queen." I got up.

"I know that." She looked up at me.

"I don't wanna hurt Sonovia." I stood her up and opened her robe.

"I know that too." She threw her head back as I traced a line from her neck down to her navel.

"Wessie..." Her stomach tightened, and I got to her pussy. She had a heart cut into her pubic area.

I raised her leg and slid my tongue up and down from her clit to her pussy hole.

"Yeeeesssss!" She grinded on my face.

I could tell the moment she was ready to cum, and I stopped.

"No, don't stop," she whined.

I picked her up and slid my tongue into her mouth with my face still wet with her cum.

"UUUUUUNNNNNNN."

Queen made a noise in my ear when my dick went in, and I couldn't help but laugh. Her shit was locked tight, and I realized she ain't had no dick in a long ass time.

"You was saving it for me?"

I watched her take the dick, and she was in another zone. The way her pussy was feeling, I would be in my own soon. I knew I should have felt bad about cheating, but man, the way I loved Queen, this shit felt right.

"I missed you so much," she moaned in my ear, and I felt her tears falling on my chest.

"I missed you too." I laid her down and pushed her legs behind her head.

All I could hear was her screams and me banging that pussy until she came back to back like rush hour. I almost didn't pull out, but I did anyway when I finally came.

"Shit." She lay on my chest, and I stared at the pool, thinking about what the fuck I had just done.

"Queen?" I heard that chick, Tevony, say before entering.

I grabbed my shirt and covered my dick.

"She cool," Queen told me.

"Sonovia Rain is out front to see you. She wanted me to make sure you heard the Rain part."

"Why is your wife at my house? Damn, she must got spidey senses," Queen said.

"What should I tell her and her brothers?" Tevony asked.

"I'll be out there in a minute." Queen looked at her then me. "This was a mistake, Wessie. I ain't no home wrecker, and even though I hate the bitch's guts, not even she deserves it," Queen said.

"I know," I said as I got dressed.

"Just wait here, and I'll get Emily to drive you home," Queen said before she walked out.

After about fifteen minutes later, Queen walked back in.

"Wessie, we finna have a big issue."

"What?" I asked.

"I'm gon' murder your wife and her brothers!" she said.

"What happened?"

"They're trying to start their own shit and take my customers. Wessie, you know I don't play about my money. I had a meeting with Carlos, Toreese, and Malcom, the one I told you about, but I guess they couldn't wait." She picked up her phone.

"Look, chill. I can't let you kill my wife, Queen," I told her.

She looked at me like, 'well, nigga, you can die with her.'

"Just go, Wessie. I knew this shit would have some type of complication. Our cum ain't even dry and look. Damn."

"Shit, you act like it's my fault."

"It's not, but they gonna be an issue. I knew that shit when Marsel left."

"Then talk to him," I told her.

"I'm sick of dealing with them through him. You know what? I ain't finna touch a hair on their heads. I don't know how they gonna get work when everybody gonna be scared to sell to them."

She was mad as shit, but I was glad I didn't have to choose Sonovia's life or Queen's. The most fucked up part is I knew it was supposed to be an easy choice since I had a wife, but it wasn't, and that was truly fucked up.

"You should go." She picked up her champagne and gulped it down.

"I'ma check on you later," I told her.

"Don't bother," she spat, and I laughed.

"I'm glad you think it's funny, Wessie." She pushed me, and I grabbed her up.

"You can be tough with everybody but me, Queen. I know you inside," I touched her pussy, "and out."

I kissed her roughly and let her go then left. I saw the chick, Erica, already sitting out front in the car, waiting for me. I got in and looked at my texts. There were several from my guys. I had to get in my mind right. I had business to take care of, and I would deal with this shit later.

Sonovia

I looked at my text from my inside connection with Queen, and when she told me that she knew Wessie and Queen had fucked when I came to talk to the bitch about our plans, I was sick. I covered my mouth and looked at the text, then locked the phone.

"Son of a bitch." I looked at the TV as the door to the suite opened.

"Who you in here cursing at?" Jacca walked in and looked confused.

"Nobody," I said as he came down and kissed me.

"You look good." He kissed my neck, and I just wasn't in the mood.

"Look, I really ain't feeling sexy right now," I told him.

"Then why the fuck you call me to meet you?" he asked.

"Because I was ready until I got a text that changed my pussy's mood. Your cousin id fuckin' Queen," I said.

"Okay, and you fuckin' me, so..." He shrugged.

"Oh my God, why would I even think you would care?" I got up, and he pulled me to him.

"I do care. I just don't see why you mad when you stepping out." He sat down and pulled out a bag of weed.

"It's her. I fuckin' hate that bitch!" I screamed, and he looked at me like I was crazy.

"Okay, and why you hate Queen so much?" he asked.

I paced and started to feel crazy, knowing she would take another nigga from me.

"This." I went to my phone and pulled up a picture of Tonka and me.

"Who these mufuckas?" he asked.

"It's me," I said.

"Huh?" He took my phone, and I smirked at his reaction.

"Damn, why you change your face? What, she beat your ass or sum?" he asked like an idiot.

"No, nigga, she killed him." I pointed to Tonka.

"Oh, damn," he replied.

"Yeah, damn. I loved him, and that bitch took his life. I fuckin' hate her." I stood and picked up my purse.

"Does Wessie know this?"

"No, he thinks it's a family beef. My real name is Qia," I told him, and he looked at me like I was one big lie.

"This shit is creepy as fuck," he stood up and said.

"Just keep your mouth closed, and don't tell Wessie shit," I warned him. Although he wouldn't be able to tell him shit anyway, I had said too much.

"I wo—" He stopped when the first bullet struck him, and the one that followed dropped his ass.

I stood over him and looked at his handsome face.

"Fucking waste of good dick," I said as I grabbed my shit.

I called my brothers and got them to come and clean Jacca up.

That's was my fault, and I felt bad that he had to die because I said shit in a fit of anger.

I got in my car and decided to show up at Wessie's favorite hangout spot. I was gonna curse his ass the fuck out.

"You wanna fuck that bitch, huh?" I said.

I saw Tonka sitting in the backseat as I looked in the rear-view mirror.

"I miss you, baby," he said.

"I miss you too, baby," I cried as he disappeared.

I often saw him and felt like maybe I was going crazy, but I figured it was because I missed him and loved him.

When I got to the bar, I saw Wessie's car out front. I knew he would be there. He had bought this place last year and spent a lot of downtime there. When I got out, I marched right through the doors and went straight up to Wessie, who was talking to his friends while watching a game on TV.

"Wessie! You fucked Queen?" I screamed.

He looked at me... well, everybody in the bitch looked at me.

"You really came in here screaming and shit like that?" He tried to calm me down.

"No, fuck you, nigga. You fucked Queen, yes or no?" I asked him.

"I fucked up, Sonovia. It was one time, shawty," he said, and I slapped him across the face.

"OOOHHHH!" some nigga yelled out.

"I knew it! That bitch always gotta have one up on me, huh?" I started to beat on his chest.

"Stop, man, what the fuck?" He held me, then I stomped his foot and broke free.

"I been fuckin' your cousin, so I guess we even!" I said, and he looked at me with squinted eyes.

I wished I could take that shit back; he wasn't supposed to know that.

Whap!

He gave me exactly what I gave him.

"So, you were a dirty bitch anyway. I'm glad I fucked her," he said in my ear, and I watched him walk out.

I looked at everyone who watched me, and I put my middle finger up.

"Fuck y'all!" I screamed and ran out.

I saw Wessie getting in his car, and I ran up.

"Get your shit the fuck out my house!" he said as he passed me.

"Our house!" I screamed behind him and wiped my eyes.

Shit, why the fuck would I say that shit about Jacca? Now, he would go trying to find him and approach him about the shit.

***

Wessie had been gone for days, and after our showdown, I didn't think he would be back. I embarrassed him and myself, and now my plan would have to move sooner rather than later. The fact that Queen fucked him let me know she was back in her feelings, and now it was time to rip her fucking heart out.

I tried to call his phone, and of course, his shit was going straight to voicemail.

"Man, shit."

I walked downstairs, and I could smell cigar smoke coming from my living room.

"The fuck." I walked in and saw my father sitting on my couch.

"Dad, what you doin' in the states?" I asked him.

"Laqia, what the fuck are you doin'?" he countered.

"I'm not doing anything."

"You killed Wessie's cousin?"

"They talk to fuckin' much," I said, speaking about my brothers.

"Nah, you need to let this bullshit go." Toreese came from the kitchen.

"Let what bullshit go?" my father asked.

"Oh, so you told him everything, but that?" I asked Toreese.

"What the fuck are y'all talkin' about?" our father shouted.

"She doing all this crazy shit to get back at Queen. She talked our stupid ass brother into leaving the organization and starting our own," Toreese said.

"So, you still stuck on this bullshit with that fuckin' loser Tonka?" he said.

My father knew that Queen killed Tonka, and he didn't care. He thought that Tonka was trash and was happy to be rid of him.

"Don't call him that," I said, feeling myself tear up.

"I let you go through your changes. When you changed your face, I said okay. When you changed your name, I said okay, but now you trying to destroy my fucking family business?" He got up.

"How is it family when a stranger is running it?" I asked him.

"You stupid ass little girl. Whatever you got planned or you been doing, let it the fuck go. That's a fucking order. I promise you don't wanna fuck with me, daughter." Dad looked at me with pity.

"You really care about that bitch more than me?" I asked as I watched him walk out.

"Nobody is leaving the organization. Your bricks come from Queen, and they will always come from her," he said to Toreese.

When they left, I texted Toreese, calling him every name but the one my mother gave his weak ass. He was always an ass kisser to our father. I called Malcom right away to warn him about what was about to come his way.

I went to close the door when it was forced back open.

"Queen, what the fuck!" I moved when two big bitches came in before she did.

"This cute." Queen looked at our house like it was shit.

"Bitch, what you doin' here?" I asked her.

"You popped up at mine, so here I am. I came to see your face." She laughed, and I wanted to knock her ass out.

"So, you ran to my father?" I rolled my eyes.

"No, the funny part about it is, your own brother came back to talk to me. I couldn't believe it. I mean, even your own brother don't fuck with you. He'd rather put up with me than to drown with you and Malcom." She lit a blunt and blew the smoke in my face. "You know, I'm gonna give you a pass on sending the niggas to fuck with Presia. Y'all knew me better than that." She stepped in my face. "Try me again, Sonovia, and I will scatter pieces of your goofy ass all over Miami, bitch."

"So, was Wessie's dick everything you remembered?" I turned my lip up.

"Then some, boo." She winked and walked back out.

"Trifling bitch. You just don't know when to leave people's niggas alone, huh?" I yelled before her security closed the door in my face in my own damn house.

I called Malcom, and he picked up.

"Leave me the fuck alone. You got me caught up in your bullshit, and now pops threatening to cut me off if I walk away. Just stop calling me!" he hung up without letting me say a single word.

I felt like everything I did was about to be destroyed.

For days I sat in the house, wondering what my next move should be when I saw a text from the same person who delivered the bad news about Queen fucking Wessie.

I covered my mouth and smirked. I wondered how on top she would feel if Wessie knew his child wasn't dead? He would hate her, and I wouldn't even have to kill him. She would be lost to him forever. I guess I had a

birthday party to crash next week. This bitch could run

everybody, but she wouldn't run me.

Queen

"So, you understand how this works?" I asked Beto one of my new customers from Peru. They had a heroin problem, and I was more than happy to supply them.

"Yes, we appreciate this so much. We got robbed, and—"

I put my hand up to stop him from talking.

"Just don't let my money get robbed, and we all good. My connect in Amsterdam has already set up a shipment, and all you need to do is be there to collect. They will only wait five minutes. If you aren't there, they will leave, and I will keep your money for my inconvenience," I told him.

"I understand." He nodded.

"Thank you." His partner kissed my hand.

"No need for thanks. Just handle your business, and we will have a long-lasting relationship," I said, and they stood up.

"Are you single?" Beto asked.

"Have a nice day," I told them as they stepped out of my office in the corporate tower that I inherited from Marsel.

He did most of his business there and rented the other suites to local businessmen.

"Damn, sis, you got a nigga tryna holla every time they make a deal." Parquita laughed.

"I'm sick of they asses." I got up. "Shit." I felt myself get dizzy and had to sit back down.

"What's wrong?" Parquita came up and handed me a bottle of water.

"I don't know. I feel sick," I told her.

"Lay down for a minute."

I lay on the couch for a while before getting up and making it out of the building.

I was feeling much better but decided to go home and relax for the rest of the day. I had handled so much today, and I just wanted to swim and relax. When I came home, I saw that Presi'sa car wasn't there, but I did see a new white Jeep in my driveway. Must have been somebody I knew because my guards would never let anyone on my property who I didn't know.

"Who dat?" Parquita looked at the car, and Vixie got her gun ready.

"Relax," I said when I saw the tag **MkitRain**.

I saw Wessie step out of the Jeep wearing shorts and a tank top. He looked angry as hell, and I wondered what the fuck the problem was.

When I stepped out, he went to his passenger side and opened the door.

"Get in," he said.

"She ain't goin' nowhere without us," Parquita said.

"Man, I got niggas who watch my back, so they watching hers too. She's good," he said her.

"Queen, you straight?" Vexie asked me.

"Yeah." I got in his Jeep, and he walked around to the driver's side.

When he pulled off, it was quiet, and I had no idea where his ass was taking me. I knew my girls, and when I saw the beamer behind me, I knew it was them.

"Tell them bitches to stop following us," he said.

I looked at him, wondering when he got so sharp. Not that he wasn't before, but he was different in some ways.

I sent a text to Vixie and told her to fall back.

"So, wassup, Wessie?"

"You don't know what today is?"

"No."

I looked at him strangely as he drove toward the beach.

"This was the last day I saw you, and the first day I met you," he said, and I was blown away that he actually remembered that.

"Damn."

"Yeah, damn. I found out Sonovia was fucking my cousin Jacca, and I'm like damn, I just keep getting fucked this month. No matter what year it is," he said.

I felt so bad because this would also be the time he believed I aborted our child.

"I'm sorry she did that to you," I said as we got caught in traffic on the bridge.

"Nah, you ain't do it this time." He chuckled. I could tell he wasn't himself right now; he was hurt.

"Where we going?" I asked.

"I don't know. I just wanted to be around you today. I just wanted to remember the day I fell in love with the shawty I fell in love with.

"Wessie, stop. You killing me," I said as I bit my lip.

"I'm just being honest. I just got a lot of shit on my mind, and I couldn't think of anyone I wanted to talk to but you." He grabbed my hand, and I looked at our interlocked fingers, remembering how it felt.

"Wessie, I got something to tell you, and I just need you to understand one more time," I told him.

"Not right now, shawty. I can't take no more shit to have on my mind. Just gimme tonight." He leaned over and kissed me.

We got to South Beach, and he let the valet park his jeep.

Wessie walked me to a small tent that looked similar to the one I always had out there.

"Oh shit." I smiled when a nigga in a suit opened the tent, and there was a table set for two.

"I thought I'd return the favor with dinner for that good ass lunch that day." Wessie pulled the chair out, and I noticed he had something over the sand.

"This is nice, Wessie." I smiled at his setup.

"You know how I do, shawty." He sat down.

We had a lobster dinner with the best Brazilian steak. That shit had me choked up, thinking about how that was Base's favorite.

We ate and lay on the beach until the sun started to set.

We ended up fucking in the tent, and I was sure that everyone who walked by could hear us.

By the time Wessie dropped me off at home, I was spent and asking him to spend the night, almost forgetting that I had Presia in my guest house.

We ended up fucking in every part of the second floor of my house, and when we finally lay down, I watched him as he went to sleep.

"I love you," I told him and gave him a kiss before I went to sleep myself.

When I woke up, he was gone. I looked for my phone, ready to curse him out for leaving without letting me know.

Wessie: *I love you too, ma.*

I held the phone to my chest and lay back. As I looked at the reminder of the birthday party in three days, I knew I had to come clean and let him know my last secret.

***

I was sick as a dog, and I felt like I needed to get my ass to a doctor.

"Queen, you gonna have to stay here and tell Tisha you can't come," Parquita said.

"Nah, we gotta go get his stuff. I ain't missing this," I said as I walked down the stairs of my house.

Tisha was throwing a big birthday party for Wesean, a child she had been raising as a favor for me. I went over there four to five times a week to spend time with him so he would always know who I was. He was only two, and since Tisha couldn't have her own children, he was a blessing in her life.

"I know, but you don't look too good." Parquita went to my kitchen and came back with water.

"I'm okay." I drunk from the bottle and closed it.

We eventually left my house, and I had Emily take me to Walmart to grab everything I ordered for Wesean. I felt so guilty about not raising my own child and even worse for letting Wessie think his child was dead. I couldn't have people targeting our son because of me, so I let my cousin look after him while I tried to make sure life was more secure. That was one of the biggest things that scared me to tell Wessie, so I let him believe what I told him, especially when I didn't think he would be back. I knew I was wrong, but I had a perfectly good reason.

When I found out I was pregnant, I told Wessie I was going to abort. I had ended up thinking it over and over until I changed my mind. So, the next day, I went to tell him that I was gonna have our baby when my girls and I caught three assassins outside of his home. Greeks. That was interesting to me because he was basically the prince of the Greek mafia. I had gone and talked to Vladimir, his great uncle, about it. Yes, I flew all the way to Greece to inquire about why they would want him dead.

Wessie had turned Vladimeer down to run the family business since he was next in line. To him, that was a slap in the face. They had a nephew who they wanted to be on the throne, but they wanted to make sure Wessie could never come back to claim it, so they put a hit on their own blood, even the sisters. That's why when Priest and Vibe mentioned Greeks, I knew they were still trying to take Wessie and his family out. When I couldn't get them to back off, I started a small war, and to protect my son and Wessie, I made sure our child wasn't known to the Greeks. All this time, Wessie had no clue how much danger he was in.

After getting all Wasean's stuff, I went to the car and saw Parquita looking like some shit had just popped off.

"What's wrong?" I asked.

"Your mother just called and said she at your cousin's house, but they aren't there," she said.

"Huh? Man, Tisha knows she gotta be there, cuz people will start showing up soon."

I took out my phone and realized it was dead. I guess that's why it made sense for Mom to call Parquita.

"I need my charger." I got in and plugged the shit up.

Once we started to drive, my phone finally turned on, and I saw a text from an unknown number. Before I got a chance to even open them, my phone was ringing from the same number. I picked up without saying anything.

"Lookin' for somebody?" I heard a female voice on the other end.

"Who the fuck is this?" I asked.

"You know I'm not gonna tell you that," she said.

Her voice didn't even sound remotely familiar.

"You looking for your son?" she asked.

"Look, I don't know who put you up to this, but I don't think you wanna play this game," I said, thinking about Tadius. I couldn't do that again.

"No, I don't think you wanna play my game, Queen. Now, if you go to Tisha's house and look in the backyard, you will find her there, but we're gonna hold on to little man for you."

"Let me guess, you want some money?" I seethed.

"No, I just want you to show your true colors." She hung up, and I screamed.

"Bruh, call everybody and tell them we got a serious situation," I told Parquita.

She picked up her phone and made the calls. When we got to Tisha's house, I saw my mother and a lot of my family out there worried.

"Did y'all check the backyard?" I asked when I got out of my car.

"Nothing back there," my mother said, looking worried.

"Somebody took Wesean," I told my mother, and she almost fell out.

"Now, I know you wanted to pretend he wasn't my grandbaby, but Queen, find my motherfuckin' grandson," she hollered and fell down.

I walked around back with Vixie and Parquita right behind me.

I looked around the backyard and didn't see shit strange until I saw the shed.

"Did y'all look in there?" I asked my cousins, and they all said no.

I walked up and figured I was being run around when I opened the shed, and nothing was there.

"Fuck."

I turned around and saw something red smeared across the small storage chest on the other end of the yard. I ran up and pulled it open then immediately slammed it back down.

"They fucking killed her!" I said, pulling my phone out when I heard it ringing.

"Bitch, you find your cousin?" the bitch said.

"Oh, you wanna die, die." I felt my face turning red.

"I'll let your son go once you tell him the truth," she said.

I looked at the phone and figure this had to be Sonovia at this point, and she was disguising her voice.

"Sonovia, I swear—"

"You swear what?" I heard Sonovia's actual voice behind me.

I saw Wessie standing in the backyard with Sonovia beside him.

"Queen, tell me she lyin' about why she brought me here," he said.

I looked at Sonovia, who had a big smile on her face.

"Wessie, you told me to wait, and—"

I felt his hands around my throat, and I was fighting him from choking me to death.

"Bitch, you kept my son from me!" he said with spit flying from his mouth.

It took everybody to pull him off me.

"Wessie, I'm so sorry." I coughed, trying to grab him as he moved away from me.

"Checkmate, bitch," Sonovia said as she walked out of the yard behind him.

"Queen, you ain't tell him about the boy?" my mother asked me.

I just got up and rushed to the front, only to see him pull off, leaving Sonovia's ass.

"Oh, what happened, bitch? Lost your ride?" I ran up and knocked her ass back with the first punch, and then I sent a barrage of punches to her face.

When she turned over to try to run, I kicked her in the ass.

"No running, bitch. This what you wanted." I kicked her in the stomach, and I felt my stomach start to hurt.

I fell on the ground and held my stomach to manage the pain.

"Queen, you aight?" Vexie ran and scooped me up. "We taking you to the hospital," she said as we got in the car.

"I gotta get my son. I can't lose another one," I cried.

"We'll get him," Parquita assured me.

When we got to the hospital, they took me straight to the back.

Once they ran all the tests, they came back and told me I had the stomach flu, which upset me because I could have spent this time trying to find my son. But when I was finally being discharged, Parquita came in with Wesean in her arms.

"They dropped him off at the police station," she told me.

I grabbed him and held him tight.

"Mommy is so sorry. I promise I won't ever leave you again."

I could tell he had no idea what was going on. I took him home and decided to put my fear of losing him aside and just hold on to him.

"We're going to go see Daddy," I told him and lay back, still holding him tightly as my tears continued to flow. I was happy to have him back.

Wessie

"Look, just 'cause you told me about my son, don't mean I want your ass. We done," I told Sonovia as I packed up more of my shit.

She could have this fucking house. I was done with this shit. Sonovia was a dirty ass bitch, and so was Queen. I was done forgiving and getting past shit. She could have let me have my child, but instead, she stashed him. Nah, that would never fly, and I wasn't fucking with her ass no more.

"Wessie, we both fucked up. You cheated too," Sonovia said.

"I don't even give a fuck. You went and fucked my blood. His pussy ass must have run, cuz I can't find him. But, like I said, fuck it. He can have you, shawty," I told her.

"Don't say that, Wessie. We married." She showed me her ring, and I tossed her the divorce papers that I had a lawyer draw up.

"Not after you sign these."

"I ain't signing shit. Where the hell you going?" She grabbed my arm.

"Don't fucking touch me!" I barked, and she jumped back.

I pulled my suitcases down the stairs, and Sid helped me load my shit into the U-Haul. I jumped in with Sid beside me and pulled off as Sonovia screamed behind me.

"Man, shawty going crazy," Sid looked in the rearview and said.

"Man, fuck her. She a fraud ass bitch. I'm sick of hoes," I said as I drove to my new house on Fisher Island.

When I opened my gate, I saw Queen sitting on my porch. I almost jumped out and screamed on her until I saw a little boy running around in the yard.

"Is that your son, nigga?" Sid asked me.

I looked at him and knew he was mine.

He ran over to Queen when I walked up. Queen looked at me then at him.

"This is Wesean," she said.

I couldn't fight back my tears.

"Come here, lil' man," I said, and I was shocked that he ran up and hugged my leg.

I saw Queen crying, and I turned from her and looked at my son.

"You know who I am?" I asked him, and he just stared.

"I'm your daddy, lil nigga." I picked him up and held him.

I was in that position for a whole five minutes before I put him down, and he started to run around again.

"You dirty, shawty," I said to Queen as I sat next to her on the porch as Wesean played without a care.

"I know, Wessie, but you don't know why," she said.

"It don't matter, ma. I'm sorry, but I can't forgive you for this shit. We can't ever be good again, Queen." I made sure she knew that before standing up and going to play with Wesean. I could tell that hurt her, and it was meant to. She couldn't hurt any worse than I was right now.

Queen stayed outside and let me spend some time with Wesean. He was a funny ass little kid, especially for a toddler. I had already made plans to set his room up for him, so I could start being a father to him the way I was supposed to be.

After they left, I called my sisters and let them know that I had got to spend time with him. Of course, Princess' sympathetic ass could only rally for me to forgive Queen.

"I don't got shit for shawty," I told her.

"Yes, you do, Wessie. I'm sure she feels like shit," Princess said.

"Good. The fuck. She had my son out here without a father. You know how I feel about that family shit. I can't let that slide."

"No, what you need to be worried about is how that bitch, Sonovia, found out about it, and why she was so eager to throw it out there. I mean, how long she knew before she told you?" Princess asked.

"Man, that ain't even the point. I'm done with her ass too, so it don't even matter.

"Man, you stubborn," she said.

"Nah, I ain't no clown. Fuck them," I said.

"Aight, bro, me and Priest finna go on our date night. Hit me," she said, and I hung up.

I was proud and happy for both my sisters. At least they got this love shit right because I obviously didn't have it in me.

When I finished moving everything in, a nigga was tired as fuck and decided to call it a night.

***

The next morning when I got up, I had two texts from Angel's crazy ass. I forgot about her for a minute because after Jacca disappeared, so did she. I still couldn't believe that nigga, but like I said, I was good. He must have run his ass back home. My phone was now ringing, and I saw that it was Marsel.

"Hello." I picked up.

"Come open the door for me," he said.

I looked at the time and wondered why the fuck this nigga was there so early. I didn't know he was still in the states.

I dragged my ass down the stairs and opened the door, letting him in along with Malcom and Toreese.

"We got a problem," Marsel said.

"What happened?" I asked.

"My daughter is in jail for two keys of coke that they found in your bathroom at the house," he said.

"What?"

"Yeah. Please tell me you weren't keeping dope where my daughter laid her head.

"Marsel, now how the fuck you comin' at me? I don't even touch dope, so why the fuck would I have it in my house?" I asked.

I had calls coming in from Angel now.

"Man, what the fuck?" I picked up. "What!" I barked.

"They found him, Wessie. They found Jacca floating in the water," she cried, and I leaned back against the door.

"You good?" Marsel asked.

"They just found my cousin dead."

"Damn, Wessie, everybody around you going down," Toreese said, and I threw a punch without even thinking.

"Aye." Marsel stepped between us.

"Look, this ain't the time for y'all fuck niggas. Marsel, you know I ain't have shit to do with that," I said.

"Let's go get her," Marsel said.

I agreed and ran up to get ready.

I looked at my phone and remembered that Angel was in my basement.

"Aye, where they find the shit at?" I ran back down and asked Marsel.

"She said the bathroom."

"I know who did it. Don't worry about it. It wasn't for her, it was for me," I told him, and we left to bail Sonovia out.

They gave me a hard time, and after a while, I realized why. She was locked up under Laqia Standfield.

"Why she under a fake name?" I asked Marsel.

"Actually, Sonovia is the fake name. She changed it a few years back. I can't believe she ain't tell you that," he said.

"Yeah, me either," I said, wondering why she would change her name.

When Sonovia came out, she ran to me and threw her arms around me.

"I'm so glad you came for me," she said.

"It's nuffin. So, you good now?" I asked.

"Yeah, just waiting on my stuff," she said.

When we go out front, I hit the remote start on my shit.

"I'm sorry about your cousin," Marsel said to me.

"Me too." I looked at Sonovia and walked down the stairs.

I didn't know why, but it was something about her changing her name that fucked with me. I wanted to check her ass out and figure out what she was hiding.

I called Angel, and she was still pretending to be hysterical. She gave me her address, and I drove over there with every intention of killing her ass. This bitch was causing too much shit, and I knew it was her who put that dope in my bathroom.

When I pulled up to her building, I saw her looking out the window. When I got to the front door, I heard a buzzing noise, and I opened it.

"Right here," she said.

I walked down, and she was in a lace set. I shook my head. This bitch probably just put this shit on for me.

"I can't believe he's gone," she said, trying to hug me.

I greeted her with a .45."

"Wessie, what the fuck you doin'?" She put her hands up.

"You planted that dope in my house?" I asked.

"I don't know what you talkin' about." She was trembling.

"You don't?" I pressed harder on her head with the butt of the gun.

"Okay, okay, it was me," she quickly said.

"You really wanna take me down that bad?" I asked.

"I was in a fucked-up space. I forgot about it, and when I saw you weren't locked up, I figured it didn't work." She got down and clasped her hands.

"I hope it was worth your life."

"I told her it was there when she came to my house. If she didn't take it out, it was because she wanted you locked up too," she said, and I put the gun down.

"She who?? I asked her."

"Your wife. She came here and threatened me. She said if I didn't help her, she would make sure Queen found out I was the one who tipped the DEA off to her. She found out, and I didn't have no way out." She cried hard.

"What?" I felt like I had no idea who the fuck Sonovia was.

"She crazy, Wessie. She didn't even look like that at first. She got her face done and shit, all cuz of Queen. She went crazy one day and told me everything. Her name used to be Qia. She was trying to kill me after she told me, but I convinced her that I was on her side, and I hated Queen too."

I looked at Angel and knew she was telling the truth.

"Well, shit, I appreciate the honesty," I told her.

She breathed a deep sigh of relief.

"Too late, though," I said.

She gasped before I let the bullet go through her skull. When she fell, I took her phone and saw that not too long ago, on the same day that I caught Queen at her cousin's house, she called Queen and blocked her number. What the fuck was going on?

Presia

"Oh, my God."

I turned around and looked at Queen behind me, licking my pussy from the back. She was so sensual with it, and I loved every minute of her. She did my body like nobody could ever. She started to bounce up and down, slurping and sucking on me until I came. Then she pushed her fingers into my pulsating pussy.

"Let me taste you, baby," I said as my orgasm subsided.

I lay on my back, and she put her pussy right on my face and started to gently bounce up and down as I stiff tongued her pussy. Queen always tasted like candy, and I loved her for that shit. She was so sweet.

I started to play with my pussy as I ate her, and her moans made me cum.

"Yes, bitch, suck this pussy." She started to ride my face until I was covered in her cum.

I pulled myself from under her, and we got into a scissor position.

"Mmmmm, fuck." I grabbed her titty as we bounced our pussies on each other until both of us came again.

"Oh my God, I love you," I told her as she smiled down at me.

She leaned down, and we kissed each other, then she got up.

I felt safe, knowing that I was staying with her temporarily until I got a new place. I was still kind of shook, and it was one more thing I had to do in order to fully commit myself to Queen.

"You know I feel worried about you stepping out. Take the gun I gave you," Queen told me as she turned her shower on.

"I know, Queen."

I kissed her, and the heaviness of the guilt I started to feel was too much. I had to free myself.

When I got dressed, Queen was already gone, and I hoped I could get myself out of this shit before she found out what the fuck was going on.

A few minutes later, I found myself sitting in my car, looking at the building that held my future. I got out and walked in, making sure nobody saw me.

"Have you lost your fucking mind?" My captain closed the door and closed the blinds when I made it to his office.

"No, but you gotta pull me out. It's too heavy for me. Some dudes came and put a gun to my head and tried to kill me!"

"Well, you know what the fuck UC means. You gotta be ready for it. You're undercover, and you're with the queen pin of fucking Miami! You think you won't be kidnapped or held hostage to get to her? If the situation was out of control, you should have blown your cover and took them down," he said.

He knew I would never do that because I had too much to prove. I had been working for the DEA just under two years, and the first case they gave me in my hometown, I fucked up and let my target find my gun and badge, so they threw me on the desk. When they came across Queen, she was untouchable, and honestly, she still is. I had never seen drugs except for the weed she and her friends smoked.

Of course, she was the Queen Malone that we were tipped off about, but we couldn't prove shit, so they put me in when they found out she liked females as well as men. They had Perry in, but all she would allow him to do was eat her pussy, and that wasn't getting us anywhere. My bosses didn't know was he was eating her pussy for his own pleasure at this point. He had been off the case, but he still went and did the shit whenever she wanted.

I hated drug dealers with a passion, and that's why I joined the force. My mother was killed just walking past the wrong building where a drug deal went bad. What was even worse was that Queen wasn't a bad person; she just chose the wrong job. I would never tell my bosses, but I had fallen in love with her, and I hated myself for it. She was a murderer and the very thing I was fighting against. I was trying to figure out a way to leave, and maybe she and I could be together.

"You can't come around here. What the hell would you do if one of her people saw you here?" Butler asked.

"Look, just take me out," I told him and opened the door to leave.

"If I take you off this case, be ready to be a permanent desk fixture," he said.

I looked at him and slammed the door. Rushing through the bullpen, I went to the elevator and took it down.

"Man, fuck." I looked at my phone and saw that I had a text on my real phone.

Colby: I know you can't see this yet, but whenever you do, I love you.

I looked at the text from my husband and laid my head in my hand. I missed him, I really did. I lived in Minneapolis, but when you go undercover with the DEA, you have to go where they tell you. I landed in Miami, and since I was still somewhat of a fresh face, I got lucky.

I wasn't even supposed to have this phone, but I couldn't just not communicate with him. I felt so guilty about enjoying fucking Queen and how I felt about her, but I still cared for him. The crazy part is, I was only supposed to be part of her team, but she instead decided to fuck me. The first time I tasted her pussy, I was hooked. I looked at the screen and just decided to call him.

"Baby, I miss you so much." He picked up right away.

"I miss you too. I don't have a lot of time. You know I'm not supposed to communicate with you, but I miss you. This case is getting harder, and I just wanna come home," I said, feeling emotional.

"I know, baby, but it's gonna be over soon. My wife is strong, and I know she got this." He hyped me up.

"Thank you, baby. How you doin' at home?" I asked him.

"I'm cool, working and missing you," he said.

"Baby, what you..." I heard a woman's voice in the background and then a door slam.

"Who the fuck was that?" I asked.

"Nobody. That was the TV, I just turned it down."

"Nigga, you think I'm slow? I know you ain't playing house with no bitch while I'm out here with my life in danger!" I couldn't believe this nigga. I had my shit, but damn, at least it was work involved.

"What the fuck was I supposed to do? You been gone a year. I was gonna put the bitch out when you came home," he said.

I hung up and stomped the phone.

"You okay?" a guy in a suit asked.

I ignored him and stomped to my car.

That's cool. Shit, maybe when we finish this case, I'll move here permanently. I could pretend to be unbothered, but I was hurt, and the fact that he had a whole plan about the shit made me sick. I wondered if he was cheating before this shit.

When I got in my car, I started it. I thought I saw something moving in my back seat, and when I tried to turn around, I felt a sharp, cold object against my neck.

"Drive," the male voice said.

"Okay."

I pulled off and tried my best to get a look in the mirror, but they kept it there and pressed harder. He told me where to turn, and we finally ended up at a car wash that looked like it was under construction.

"Okay, look, I don't know you, but I got money in the bank. I can give you whatever you want." I told him.

"Take the keys out and toss 'em back here," he demanded.

He got out, and I saw that there was a voice box on the mask. When he took the mask off, it was Parquita. She opened the door and pulled me out.

"What the fuck?" I looked at her when she put me down.

"Why you at the DEA office?" I heard Queen, and I almost pissed my pants.

"Huh?" I felt my knees wobbling.

"Bitch, you conscious, so I know you can hear me," she said. "I put security on you this morning when you left to protect you in case anything else popped off. They followed you there, so what the fuck was you doin' there, Presia?" she asked me again.

"Listen, Queen, can we go talk? I can explain everything." I walked up to her, and she slapped me so hard I felt like my jaw was loose. "You trying to snitch on me." She put a gun to my head.

"Oh my God, no, Queen, please." I got on my knees and begged for my life.

"Tell me why I shouldn't," she said, and I grabbed her leg.

"I'm an undercover DEA agent." I dropped my head.

"Snake ass bitch. So, when I looked into your background, all that shit was made up? You fuckin' rat." She slid the gun back.

"I can help you." I looked up at her, and she looked down at me like I was dog shit.

"How?"

"I can get your case closed. I can jus—"

She let a shot off by my ear.

I screamed and dropped.

"You got five more seconds to tell me why I shouldn't kill your ass," she said.

"I told them I didn't wanna do it anymore because of how I felt about you. I don't wanna see you in jail." I talked quickly.

She looked at me, and I hoped she knew how sincere I was.

"You know what? You can be helpful." She put the gun down.

"Man, fuck that shit, Queen. Kill this bitch," Parquita said.

"No, I need a favor." Queen squatted and got in my ear. "If you fuck me and try to run to your fed homeboys, I'm gonna kill your ass and anybody else you know in your real life and this fake one."

She got up and allowed me to get off the floor.

"I need you to find out who's been driving this car." Queen gave me the tag number.

"Okay, then I'll disappear, and you won't see me again," I told her.

"Be careful what you wish for." She punched me in the face over and over again until I fell to the ground.

"That's for having me worry about your ass when you were trash anyway, I should have let them kill your ass." She spit on me and then stepped over me.

"Don't disappear just yet." Queen got in her car, and they pulled off.

"Fuck."

I got up and grabbed the keys from the backseat, then looked in the mirror and saw that my shit was knotted up. Damn, I liked it better on her good side.

***

I couldn't believe I fucked up like this and blew my cover anyway. Now I was gonna have to run after this shit I was doing for Queen. I hoped she didn't take the information and kill me anyway. Then, if they found out I was helping her and using the agency to do it, I would go to jail.

I just wished Queen would hear me out. I would take all the shit talking and everything just for her to forgive me and let me be under her again.

"You eating?" the one-eyed white woman came up with her order pad in hand.

"Yeah, I'll take a coffee and a stack of blueberry pancakes."

"Alright." She walked off, and I saw Pierre walk in the diner.

"Hey." I waved, and he walked up with a scowl.

"You call me while you're undercover?" he said through clenched teeth.

"I fucked up. I need your help," I told him, and he shook his head.

"I knew you would fuck this up. I knew it. I said be a nurse or anything else, but don't do this." He waved the waitress over.

"I'll take orange juice and blueberry pancakes," he told her.

"Wow, you both ordered the same thing." She giggled.

"He had my mother make them every morning." I looked at my father.

I never called him dad because he didn't want us to. My father was Pierre Coach, and he was the director of the FBI's Intelligence unit. He was a real hard ass and resented my sisters and me for not being boys.

"What you get yourself into?" he asked me.

"I need you to use that software and find pictures of this car." I took the piece of paper out and handed it to him. "This is the tag number."

"Why can't you do it through your own channels?" he asked.

"Because I blew my cover by going to the DEA building. She had people following me."

"Then you need to pull out right now. I'm gonna call a friend," he said.

"No. She would kill me. I know she could find me."

"Then, if she threatened, you get her locked up. I don't get why this is so hard."

"Here you go." Our waitress came and put our food on the table and our drinks.

She walked off, and we waited until she was out of earshot before either of us spoke again.

"So, who tag is this?" he asked.

"I don't know, Daddy. Please, just find out."

I was on the verge of tears, and I must have been a wreck to call him that. I was afraid to die, and after my betrayal, I knew that was coming, but if I could stop it by doing this one thing, I would do it.

"Okay, but you better call me the minute you ready to leave." He started to eat.

We ate in silence, and he sent a text out with the tag. Before we left, he had images caught by camera lights and government buildings where the tag had hit. Technology was amazing, and he sent me all the images. After he left, I sat there for a minute and looked at the hundreds of pictures and realized I only had pictures of the car until I got one where somebody was getting out of it. I flipped the next picture and scrunched my face up. I zoomed in on the picture and realized who I was looking at.

I called Parquita. Since Queen had blocked my calls, I had to go through her.

"Wassup, shorty?" She picked up.

"I got the picture of the chick driving the car," I told her. "It's—"

"Shut up! Fuck you talkin' on the phone and shit for." She hung up and sent me a text to meet her.

I drank down my coffee and got up.

I walked out of the diner and followed the directions to a small apartment building. I saw niggas sitting out front and grabbed the gun Queen had given me when she still cared. I sent her a text right before, even though I knew she wouldn't get it.

Me: I'm so sorry I lied and deceived you. Believe me when I say I love you, Queen. I did what you asked, and I'm meeting Parquita now. If you have any compassion for me left, please forgive me.

Love, Sharmaine.

I used my government so she could know who I really was. I got out and walked past the guys and into the building to the door in the text. After I knocked, I waited for the door to open. My father had sent me more messages. I looked through them and knocked on the door again. Then I got to the picture where two women were getting in.

"Oh shit," I said.

When I looked up, the door was open, and Parquita stood there with a gun to me.

"You?" I put my hands up. She was the second woman in the picture.

"Us." Sonovia stepped from behind her.

"Why would you do this to Queen?" I looked at Parquita, knowing how much Queen loved her as a sister.

"I guess you won't ever know. Kill her, baby." Sonovia kissed Parquita.

She shot me in the stomach, and I fell down.

"If you got Wessie like that, we wouldn't be worried about Queen," Sonovia said as Parquita stood over me and shot me again in the chest.

I felt myself go.

To be continued

CPSIA information can be obtained
at www.ICGtesting.com
Printed in the USA
LVHW091819211119
638113LV00005B/913/P